The Dark Angel

Best Kept Secret of World War II

Antonio M. Calabretta

All rights reserved. This book or parts thereof may not be reproduced in any form, stored in any retrieval system, or transmitted in any form by any means—electronic, mechanical, photocopy, recording, or otherwise—without prior written permission of the author, except as provided by United States of America copyright law.

Copyright © 2018 Antonio M. Calabretta

All rights reserved.

ISBN: 1983478156
ISBN-13: 978-1983478154

The sweetest smiles hold the darkest secrets
-- Sara Shepard, Flawless (2007)

PROLOGUE

1942. The second world war rages between the Axis and Allied Powers. Daniel, a skilled navigator in the German navy, has done everything asked of him for his country and is called upon one last time for a top-secret mission that leads him deep into enemy territory. His family is left in the dark regarding his whereabouts, and he's left in the dark regarding the particulars of the mission. But should he succeed, he'll finally have a chance to see them again. But tragedy soon finds him: aboard a ship with no communication gear, his fate nearly sealed when he and his commanding officer, Colonel Ziegler are taken prisoner and kept at the behest of their captors, chances of Daniel seeing his family again are all but gone.

With their hands tied in the custody of the enemy and without a means of contacting German high command, Daniel and Ziegler must find a way to preserve the secrecy of their mission without compromising their own lives. However, as pressure mounts around them and the stakes rise, a deep web of secrets begins to unravel and the harsh reality of the German's mission threatens to reshape the world as they know it.

CONTENTS

I	*Somewhere in Northern Atlantic Ocean*	7
II	*Somewhere in Greenland*	17
III	*Somewhere in Northern Atlantic Ocean*	21
IV	*Somewhere in Greenland*	31
V	*Somewhere in Northern Atlantic Ocean*	33
VI	*St. Tropez, Southern France*	42
VII	*Santiago Island, Cape Verde*	44
VIII	*Downtown Manhattan, New York City*	47
IX	*Santiago Island, Cape Verde*	52
X	*Santiago Island, Cape Verde*	62
XI	*Somewhere in Greenland*	72
XII	*Downtown Manhattan, New York City*	75
XIII	*Some Island Ashore of the Eastern US Coast*	80
XIV	*Kiel, German Naval Base*	89
XV	*Some Island Ashore of the Eastern US Coast*	116
XVI	*Somewhere in Northern Atlantic Ocean*	123
XVII	*Somewhere in Greenland*	129
XVIII	*Somewhere in Greenland*	133
XIX	*Somewhere in Greenland*	136
XX	*Somewhere in Greenland*	138
XXI	*Lisbon, German Embassy*	142
XXII	*Somewhere in Greenland*	144

CHAPTER I

SOMEWHERE IN NORTHERN ATLANTIC OCEAN

A bright, red fire burned crisp tobacco leaves. They had been packed loosely, without much concern for quality, but the potency of the leaves more than made up for the shoddy craftsmanship of the cigarette. Smoke billowed from the tip of the cigarette, and the red fire regressed inwards towards where Daniel's pointer and middle fingers clutched the tube. White-gray ash fell from the end, fragmenting into pieces as the wind carried it out to the sea.

It didn't matter how many times he'd been on the boat or how triumphant they'd sailed away from another campaign. Nothing ever seemed to dull the aching in his chest knowing his son was at home without his father, growing up and experiencing more of the world. He was three now and though not yet old enough for his formative memories to solidify, there were still educational rifts the boy would have. Daniel tried to tear his mind from the thought. He inhaled deeply and watched as the flame consumed the rest of the cigarette. It burned only a few centimeters from his fingers. He felt the heat tear at his skin.

With a flick, he discarded the cigarette into the sea. Smoke crept slowly from his nostrils. It had been a while since they'd allowed him out into the open air. He'd been fascinated with the stars for as long as he could remember. It was only by his obsession with them that the U-boat deemed him worthy to take him along on their military campaigns. To them, his value began and ended with navigation. But navigation was as far as his expertise went. He couldn't read the date in the stars. Without calendars or computers on board, he couldn't say for sure, although it must have still been April. "It's Tuesday," Daniel said to himself with a smile despite having no way of knowing for sure. The thought brought him some peace.

"Daniel Sommer can read stars." That's how his fellow Germans introduced him to other soldiers or higher ups in the rare moments that they were allowed a social pause. He appreciated their need of him. It was that need that kept him employed—that put food on the table for the boy he left at home. But it all felt peculiar. Even among his people, he was an outcast; Daniel retreated from the conning tower, slightly. Then he remembered. He couldn't leave. He had no true freedoms on his boat. He reached a hand into his breast pocket and produced another cigarette. He lit it by match and puffed wearily. Some of the sailors were on rotation overnight to ensure the ship didn't strike an iceberg. The man whose responsibility that current was needed to take a break to use the restroom, so it fell upon Daniel to temporarily oversee his post. But then, the soldier had been gone for so long, Daniel fear he'd been duped. And it wasn't as though Daniel could step away. *Someone* had to stay up there and keep the boat clear of any obstacles. He puffed on his cigarette once more.

The war had worn men down. They'd lost their fair share of conflicts by charging in overzealous and facing the business ends of primed rifles. Russia and the United States in particular had hammered several significant German operations into dust. People were starting to lose faith in high command's zeal for heavy assaults. Their new doctrine mandated stealth over super-aggression. For seamen, that meant lowering detectability. The U-boat Daniel was stationed too lacked most of the modern technology invented for the sole purpose of simplifying naval navigation. Radar and radio, and all the rest of the electronic equipment sailors were trained to operate, had no place on their vessel. Instead, they relied on Daniel alone to keep them moving in the right direction, and thus far, he'd completed his task admirably.

During the day, he slept. During the day, the boat submerged itself in full stealth mode, sneaking through the waters towards classified targets. At least one guard would be posted outside of Daniel's quarters, armed and on orders to disable Daniel should he attempt to leave his quarters without prior authorization. It felt less than official, as though he'd been taken as a hostage to his own state, but he understood the necessity: compartmentalization of information; He lacked the rank to be privy to information that was common knowledge to most all else on the boat. He wasn't that important.

Below, the waves brushed against the sheeny finish of the

boat. By nighttime, they could rise above the water so that the boat could recharge itself. Whatever mechanisms were in place that allowed the boat to gather that kind of energy, Daniel imagined, was also classified because nobody had bothered to explain the details of the boat's operation to him. A familiar rage spiked in him.

He knew little of the boat or of the missions, but he knew that Greenland was not far from their current position. And he knew at that longitude, the water would be bitterly cold. Every seaman knew the longitudes where hypothermia would be an issue, but it still got hammered into all of them before the boat departed. He'd float on the surface of the water like an ice cube, bobbing up and down as the waves struck him. There would be little struggle. With waters that cold, moving the body becomes difficult. Without training and a strong will, there would be no resistance.

Daniel questioned how much will he would have. Then he thought of his son and he knew that he would have enough. Perhaps not enough to avert the hypothermia, but enough to resist. Enough to put up a good fight. But that was an enemy he could not afford to engage.

"Damn the war," he mused aloud, taking a long drag from his cigarette. "Excuse me?" The words came in a thick German accent and from a voice so sharp and self-important that it could only belong to one man. Cristoph Ziegler. He stepped up besides Daniel and placed one hand on the railing. With the other, he gestured for a cigarette. Daniel complied, pulling the last of his hand rolled stock from his pocket and offering it to his commanding officer.

"I miss my son," Daniel replied in his native tongue. It was the truth and the best reason he could think of to have openly decried the war.

"English, please. This is a private conversation.", Most of the crew couldn't speak or understand English well, but Cristoph was the exception. He had worked as a military interpreter and had been sent on numerous classified missions to eavesdrop. When he spoke English, his German accent was largely put on. He was the kind of man who never showed his full hand, not even when he was down to the last card. Even the general under whom he served, Von Kleist, could not vouch for Cristoph's full range of specializations. The same could not be said about Daniel. Cristoph knew all he needed to know including that Daniel's studies had taken him to England where he fluently learned the language. Between the two of them, it was the easiest code to speak in, if necessary.

"We all miss our children. And our families. I have learned to cope with their absence. You should learn the same."

"When we get back to Germany—", "I'm afraid you might be disappointed."
Daniel turned and raised an eyebrow. "Why would you say that?"

"When we return home, I regret to inform you that none of us are permitted to contact our families." Cristoph turned away from Daniel. "This is a mission of the utmost secrecy.

The Abwher must confirm that the details of this mission were not compromised before we may be reunited with our families."

"Aren't you forgetting that I don't know anything about the mission?" Daniel's chest rose and fell fervently. He tried his best not to let Cristoph sense his discontent, but the anger hung on his every word; "No. And you'll be better off forgetting that there even is a mission here. At any rate, we must take these precautions for your own safety."

What seemed like a lifetime ago, the secret service snatched Daniel from his official post. It had been only a few days from his return home to see his family. He had been counting the hours when they stole him away in the dead of the night to serve a new purpose. He had pleaded then and many times after, but no one cared that his wife and son mourned his absence. They'd allowed him to write them a letter before dispatching him on their stealth U-Boat. And now, this. Heat built up in him, and tears formed at the corners of his eyes.

But he would not show his commanding officer that weakness. He refused to. It wasn't his war to fight, but he understood very well what malicious punishments the Nazi party executed against defectors—even *potential* defectors—in the past. He couldn't bear the thought of losing his life to men serving the country he loved. Nor could he ever forgive himself if he left his wife and son to live without him, completely unaware of the truth surrounding his disappearance. It was those thoughts that kept Daniel from speaking his mind.

Despite his effort though, Cristoph read between the lines. "You have served with a spotless record since you enlisted. It would be a pity if you didn't see it through to the end that way."

Daniel clenched his fists. Both he and Cristoph knew it wasn't by enlistment that he came to become an army man. He was conscripted, stolen from a perfect life for one of lies. He never felt particularly strongly about the Nazi party; his were not always popular opinions, but he always knew how to keep them to himself. That changed from the moment of his enlistment. Every day felt like a waltz through a minefield. Today was one of those days when a wayward step brought him too close to one of those mines.

"Do you ever think there may have been someone more qualified than me for this? Someone who knew more about naval procedure?"

"I've already explained to you. Information must be compromised. Anyways, you *weren't* the first choice. Not at all. Two came before you. Both died."

The heat building in Daniel came to a stop. A chill replaced it. "Died?"; "An air strike for the most recent one, just before we were to meet me to inform him of his mission."

They took the easy way out, Daniel thought. He turned to look over the railing and out into the sea where waves stretched for miles in every direction. "You no doubt wish something of that sort will happen to me."

"Ah, and now you confuse first choice with best choice."

Whatever the reason for Daniel being there, he could not reconcile his position with his beliefs. But then he saw his wife's face, and his son's after that, and everything ahead of him became clear. He knew perfectly well what was required of him: blending in. Maintaining the façade guaranteed his life, and only then could he return home; Somewhere in the distant horizon, his family waited on shore; And somewhere in the near horizon, a sharp point bobbed above the water. For a solid minute, Daniel focused on that point, transfixed by its exponential growth. It did not move from side to side, nor did it move organically. However, it grew wider as the tip rose towards the clouds. The point gained its true form.

"Iceberg!" Daniel shouted out to the sea. Then, realizing his voice would not carry, turned back inwards to the ship and declared the same. "Turn the ship!"

Cristoph looked baffled. He immediately made for the crew's quarters. "Turn the ship!" Daniel yelled again.

But it was too late. The speed with which they approached the iceberg could not be slowed—not fast enough. The movement Daniel *did* feel was not at all what he'd expected. He thought the submarine would turn sharply and steer at least partially clear of the iceberg. Instead, he heard the engine lurch and the ship slowly jeering right. It did slow down, but that was the worst thing it could have done, because it lost all its maneuverability. If they'd sped into the turn, they might have cleared the iceberg, but now there would be no hope for them. Daniel thought they'd collide with it for sure now. Most of the crew slept soundly, and by the time word got around to wake them all, tragedy would have already fallen upon them. Daniel understood this as well as anyone else, born sailor or not. He could only watch in awe as the chunk of ice grew larger and larger, and the full scope of their peril came into the light. Several moments later, Cristoph returned to his side, hopelessly out of breath.

"There's nothing to be done," he panted, eyes stricken with horror. "It doesn't look like any of us will be making it back to Germany, my friend."

It was the first time Cristoph had ever regarded him as an equal. No doubt, the prospect of an impending death softened his Nazi harshness. Daniel nodded absent-mindedly. Reflected in the sheet of ice, now mere meters from the hull of their ship, he saw the face of his wife and child—at least, he thought he saw as much—both of them smiling at him. Daniel smiled back at them and closed his eyes.

Ice tore through the ship, splitting the hull in two. Water immediately splashed onto the deck. Screams of sailors below resounded through waves of water. Like a backdraft, the waves poured in to the openings rent by the collision of the iceberg. Daniel and Cristoph both, from their privileged position, felt little of the immediate repercussions. They were saved from a quick and violent death, but the sheer force of the collision tossed them both against the railing.

Cristoph wailed as he flipped over. His arms flailed randomly in search of a support. Two fingers caught on to the railing. Then, they promptly slipped, and Daniel watched his commanding officer descend down into the cold waters.

Hypothermia, Daniel thought as he too rammed against the railing. A throb pulsed at his skull. Even in the darkness of night, his surroundings became noticeably darker. Sound exited from his ears. For a moment, all his sense shut down. Then he felt the cold of the surface of the water, and the rush of ocean folding over him.

Submerged. Freezing. He saw them again, his family, suspended just above the surface of the water and reaching down to him. They smiled, two sharp points of light. But that light could not last. It could not penetrate the darkness of the ocean's depths.

CHAPTER II

SOMEWHERE IN GREENLAND

Olaf recalibrated the machine for the third time, marking on a sheet of paper the exact specifications for future reference. There was never any telling how long they'd be on any site, so it always paid off to have the calibrations recorded to match whatever material they'd be digging through. In this case, it was one of Olaf's least favorite: ice. The thing with ice is that it was incredibly easy to miss the mark by a few centimeters, then walk away thinking you'd spent the last few weeks chasing after ghosts. The oil, after all, couldn't flow through those two centimeters to let you know it was there. Digging through dirt was much different because the oil would frequently leak from either the bottom or the sides of wherever the drill was positioned. But with ice, everything had to be perfect. You had to know exactly where to look.

In that regard, Olaf was lucky. The company insisted that every particular be attended to in a precise order. It was the ultimate efficiency machine, and Olaf just happened to be on the far end of it. All the work that preceded his made the dig exponentially simpler. Everything from current physical properties to past history, he made sure to study intensely. Or rather, he'd have someone else do the legwork, but it was all company policy. That research data was strewn out on a folding table next to the drill console. It was because of that research that Olaf could quickly calibrate the drill as many times as he did.

With the device properly calibrated, Olaf hovered over the control panel for a while, then pressed the start button. The drill screeched to life, piercing through the ice, and slowly bearing deep into the ground. The noise was incredibly loud, but Olaf had done it so many times before, he could numb himself to the noise. He watched over it wistfully, waiting for the drill to complete its descent. In less than a minute, it did just that. The spinning drill slowed its rotation to a stop. Next to the drill button was another which would insert a metal rod into the ice. That rod would be what extracted any oil, liquid or gas. He pressed it and immediately a sound like crashing thunder sent vibrations through the ice.

For this, Olaf had covered his ears. It didn't matter how many times he'd heard it. A sound like that would be the death of your ears without the proper precautions.

It repeated multiple times, alternating between the drilling and the hammering until, quite unexpectedly, the noise stopped. Olaf stepped forward slightly. Indeed, the drill wasn't moving. On the console, he couldn't see any signs that it had reached anything worthwhile. The drill LED was still lit green.

"Ah, what the hell," he muttered. He held down the

manual override button on the machine, and the drill screeched. He didn't need to hold it much longer to know he'd hit something, though it wasn't at all what he wanted. "Wasn't in the reports. Shouldn't be any rock here."

The research had never been wrong—well, up until then, it hadn't. Olaf had little mind to deal with it, but what choice did he have? As quickly as he could eject the drill, he did so. This was followed by further recalibrating, and the attachment of a shaving tool to the end of the drill.

It was a flat, rotating blade designed specifically to cut away at ice. He positioned the drill in the same place and began the laborious process of whittling away the ice.

Olaf worked at this for a little over an hour when the rock he thought he found revealed himself to be something else entirely. The rotating blade sparked against a metal sheet.

"What do we have here," he whispered, ejecting the drill once more. He stepped closer to the section he'd cut out—roughly a yard in diameter—to run his hands over the base of the metal sheet. Through the unshaved ice, he could approximate how far the metal sheet extended. It moved parallel to the surface of the ice, slowly slanting downward to a point beyond which Olaf could not see.

Close to where the metal sheet *was* visible, however, Olaf could make out what appeared to be a symbol of some sort, a crooked cross by his estimation. He strained to better decipher what the symbol was to no avail. The ice distorted the image too heavily for him to be certain of anything.

Now driven by curiosity, he re-primed his instruments and began anew with whittling away the ice. In considerably less time than the first shave, he unearthed another segment of the metal sheet. Enough was visible for him to make out the symbol. A crooked cross, indeed.

Olaf had stumbled upon the remains of a Nazi construct. Against the worn, grey metal, that black swastika endured with all its boldness.

CHAPTER III

SOMEWHERE IN NORTHERN ATLANTIC OCEAN

Soft, angelic voices whispered fragmented sentences in the distance. Daniel couldn't quite understand them—he couldn't even say for sure what language they were speaking. His head felt mostly at easy except for the wavy sensation that plagued him since regaining consciousness. He was grateful to feel anything at all, even the most uncomfortable bits. After what had happened on the boat, he hadn't expected to wake up again. The cold, hypothermic waves had buried him. It was a miracle that he still lived.

Daniel struggled to swivel his head. Throbs of soreness beat at his head and chest and were exasperated by every movement. Still, he bore the worst of it to observe the room he'd awoken in. Everything from the walls to the furnishings to the door appeared non-distinct. In his current state, Daniel couldn't tell if it was because the room was really incredibly plain or if the fogginess in his mind simply prevented him from seeing the world as it was. He quickly gave up on trying to determine his location. But before his eyes fluttered back close, he turned the other way and saw something that gave him a little more hope for his circumstances.

Cristoph lay in a bed adjacent to his own, chest steadily swelling. He was alive. At the very least, the threat of hypothermia had been avoided. They'd both survived the fall, though nothing could be said of the other members of the crew. Daniel strained again to hear the whispering voices, which now sounded more sinister than angelic. For certain, the language was unfamiliar to him.

Russian, he thought in a moment of panic and fell back into unconsciousness.

* * *

"Daniel? Daniel. Get up.'", Daniel roused from his sleep and immediately gave in to a fit of panic: "They're going to kill us" he said, he leapt from bed and straight into Cristoph who stood at its edge. Cristoph then clutched his underling by the shoulders to hold him steady.

"Quiet. Don't make such a noise. From here on out, you need to do exactly what I tell you to do. Do you understand?" Daniel blinked rapidly. His head, much clearer than it had been earlier, now swiveled without pain. He could pinpoint the details of the walls surrounding them. There were few. Gray metal on all four sides with no windows. The door appeared to be thicker than the surrounding walls and, to Daniel's discomfort, had neither a handle nor a knob. It could only be opened from the outside.

"I asked you a question, soldier.", "Yes!" Daniel answered in a heavy breath. His chest heaved at the thought that they'd been captured by the enemy. His family would never know what happened to him. They'd wait years to hear news of his return. Eventually, the war would end; their expectation would turn into inconsolable grief. There would not be a soul on the earth from whom they could hear the truth of Daniel's demise.

"Judging from your face, I can tell you've come to the same conclusion I have."; Daniel barely registered that he was supposed to be having a conversation. His concentration all focused on fantasizing about the future wretchedness of his family, Cristoph continued: "We're being kept captives—", "The Russians got us. They're going to kill us. I've heard the stories. The torture. The brutality.".

Cristoph replied sharply: "Do you really think we'd be alive if this was a Russian facility?"

But nothing short of an answer from the source could bring Daniel peace. He fell backwards onto his bed and buried his face in his hands.

"If you put your ear to the far wall, you can still hear the sound of the ocean. We're still at sea, probably on the vessel of a neutral power. Otherwise, we would not be allowed these pleasantries. Prisoners of war do not enjoy the comfort of beds."

Now Daniel's breathing began to slow. He removed his hands from his face and stood up again. "Okay…okay, that makes sense. You're right. But if it isn't the Russians who captured us, then who?", "That's what I intend to find out."

Boldly as a free man, Cristoph approached and knocked on the door. At first, no answer came, so he knocked harder. This time, there was audible muttering, and someone finally opened the door. The first thing Daniel noticed was the barrel of a rifle slowly come into view as the door opened. He wasn't a trained soldier, only a valuable navigator. The sight of the weapon caused him more discomfort than he would ever admit, but Cristoph maintained his composure even when the gun came into full view and a second armed man entered the room. He used his rifle to motion Cristoph backwards.

The two began speaking to one another, each in their native language. Needless to say, the conversation ended quickly and delineated into a series of gestures between the two. By the end of it all, the armed men disappeared back behind the door.

"Come, Daniel." The Major neither made eye contact nor directed Daniel where he was supposed to go. They were trapped in a cell with no way out. While Daniel pondered his directions, Cristoph went quick to work with pulling out drawers, checking under the beds and mattresses, tearing apart whatever he could for answers. Starved for something to occupy his own time in captivity, Daniel joined in the search. On the far side of the wall, a metal wardrobe was very slightly ajar. This was Daniel's first destination, and when he pulled open the hanger, he smiled at what he saw.

"Cristoph, sir! Look!" Daniel felt a hand grip his shoulder

and tear him to the side. Cristoph laughed triumphantly.

"Good, good. They are still a little wet, but we can work with this. Perhaps they will not speak with half-nude men, but they will respect the authority of fellow servicemen." He quickly grabbed his own uniform and began to dress himself.

Was it really such a good idea to antagonize their captors? Daniel saw nothing good coming of Cristoph's plan to negotiate. He was a privileged man, used to having his way. The way he scrambled after first contact with the guards, it was evident captivity didn't suit his sense of grandeur. Daniel, though, only felt the need for self-preservation, and so far their captors had done nothing to bring them any harm. They'd been nothing but helpful, saving them both from a death at sea.

"Daniel!" Cristoph barked. He held up the familiar shirt. "Uniform."; "With all due respect, sir, maybe it's not the best idea to do this.", Cristoph pushed the uniform against Daniel's naked chest. "Put it on, soldier."

Even in captivity, the hierarchy reigned. Daniel did what was asked of him. A few minutes after the two of them got dressed, Cristoph cleared his throat.

"We are not in a good situation, not at all. German high command needs to be made aware of our situation. It is imperative that they know some of us still live.", "German high command," Daniel scoffed. "Do you never think about your family or the things you love? We could die here, and the only thing you care about is the mission."; "Because, Daniel, I am mature enough to understand that the only thing that matters *is* the mission. You will never see your family again if we fail, and the mission asks us to succeed. So you tell me: which of us has the better perspective?"

Daniel shrunk where he stood. Maybe for someone like Cristoph who willingly enlisted, that kind of thinking could help him through tough situations, but when you didn't have a choice, everything looked different. Daniel saw everything he cared about reflected all around him. The images of everything he stood to lose haunted him. But not Cristoph. Even their prison was a warzone. He pressed his ear against one of the walls, listening intently for who-knew-what. When the back wall against which their beds were propped (the wall most likely settled against the ocean) produced nothing of value to him, he checked the right wall.

"What are you doing?" Daniel asked, "Shh, shh. I hear them. We are not alone." Though skeptical of the use of eavesdropping through the walls, Daniel knelt down beside Cristoph and placed his ear to the wall; There it was. Muffled voices vibrated against the wall. "…been sunk…swarm…boats…" The men spoke in English, likely British officers judging from the accents. But they didn't say anything incredibly revelatory until the word *German* popped into the conversation. Instinctively, Cristoph and Daniel both pressed their ears harder against the wall. "whole bloody pack…survive…us…"

A tinge of happiness found its way into Cristoph's eyes. "Shows those Allied bastards right. Looks like our U-boats are superior to their submarines. From the sound of things, we made quick work of them."

Daniel was just about to protest when there came a rap at the door. Before either of them could answer, the door opened and two uniformed men entered the room. The door was promptly shut; That's when the Germans exhaled in relief. These men wore the uniforms of their state. Portuguese, not Russian. Daniel recognized the flag patches sewn into their uniforms. While German education didn't pay specific attention to other nations, Daniel had studied in England for a short while and learned the flags of a good number of European countries. But just because the men were Portuguese didn't mean they were out of the frying pan just yet—there could have very well still been a fire burning beneath them.

One of the two officers steps forward; "High rank," Cristoph whispered, pointing at the insignia on the officer's shoulder, the officer began speaking, rather quickly. Cristoph strained to try to pick out cognates, but his panicked expression revealed his failure in that regard. When the officer finished speaking, he turned to the officer behind him, who now stepped forward.

Cristoph opened his mouth to speak but was interrupted by the second officer, who spoke in perfect German.

"You are aboard a vessel of the Portuguese navy. We found you floating out by the wreckage of what we assume was your ship." Daniel caught subtle spite in the man's voice. "We have rescued many sailors from the wreckage of ships destroyed by U-boats. In fact, we were only out here to lend support to one of our own after receiving an SOS. You are the only German survivors we have found in our waters. Admittedly, this pleases me, but it is not in my nature to leave shipwrecked sailors to their deaths.", the ship's captain spoke a little more, then motioned his translator.

"We have rescued Canadians. Brits. Americans. You are all kept separate from each other to prevent hostilities on this ship. I'm sure they'd all love to get their hands on you, but as a neutral party in this war, we have no intention of being the staging ground for your conflict."

Daniel turned to face Cristoph who, for the first time, seemed truly distressed, "I demand to speak with German command immediately. Tell your commander that." Cristoph's voice was cold.

The translator conveyed the message at which the captain chuckled. He spoke more in Portuguese. His translator nodded solemnly at the end of every sentence.

"Well?" Cristoph stepped forward aggressively. It was only by Daniel's quick reaction, raising an arm to obstruct his movement, that a confrontation didn't ensue.

"You have no identifying garments. Unless you'd like to verify your name and rank—", "Colonel Cristoph Zeigler of the German Army; Daniel stepped forward. "And I am—" "Quiet. I am the officer of rank here." Then Cristoph looked back to the Portuguese sailors. "Let me speak with my commander."

The translator conveyed the message at which the captain

laughed. He gave an amused response: "What is your unit?" The translator asked. "And what were you doing in those waters?", Cristoph reply came sharp as a knife: "I could ask you the same question. A bit far north for Portugal."

"I'll start then. We're transporting medical supplies to help the war effort. As you can imagine, we must protect those supplies." The translator pointed his finger and pulled it back like a gun. "Now then. What were *you* doing there?"; Cristoph scoffed. "I am not at liberty to disclose."

"*Ich auch nicht.*" The captain responded. An in-depth response to his translator followed.

"You absolutely will not be in contact with your commanding officer, not until we have safely reached our destination. Understand that this is for the safety of all the sailors we have rescued. When we reach Cape Verde, feel free to make another request. Depending on our situation, it may be permitted."

Fury grew in Cristoph's eyes. Daniel kept his arm raised, occasionally resisting the forward force his superior exerted. He wanted to get in contact with another German as much as anyone else, but he despised conflict. Conflict was the reason he'd been whisked away from the ones he loved. In a situation like they were currently in, more conflict would only exasperate the matter. They needed to stay calm.

The translator continued after a short conversation with the captain. "Until further notice, you are to stay confined in this room. Food will be brought to you." He then gestured to a hidden compartment on the wall of the room. "There is a latch. If you pull the wall out, you will find a toilet. Make yourself comfortable. The captain also wants you to know that none of the other sailors are being permitted to contact their people either. We have done you all a service by rescuing you. The only alternative was your death, so we only ask that you cooperate for as long as we need you to. You will have an opportunity to contact your people when it is safest."

The two Portuguese men didn't waste any more time in the room. They departed before Cristoph could get another word in, clicking the lock behind them. Everything seemed to get colder. Their situation, of course, had been made better by the revelation of their circumstances. Daniel still couldn't express properly how relieved he was that they weren't captured by Russians. Cristoph, though, refused to settled for good news unless it was the precise news he wanted. Even in their perilous situation, he kept the details of the secret mission just that: secret. His fury must have been related to that somehow, but Daniel could only wonder.

However, in that moment, it didn't matter to him. He returned to his bed, wrapped himself in the covers, and closed his eyes. Meanwhile, Cristoph still stood in the middle of the room with his fists clenched, staring vacantly at the locked door.

CHAPTER IV

SOMEWHERE IN GREENLAND

It didn't take long for others to arrive to help with the excavation. Since he'd already worked all day, his coworkers refused to let Olaf lift a finger in the digging that followed. So he watched from the outskirts as the metal plate he initially unearthed grew in size and altered in shape. The men dug throughout the day, eventually uncovering a good deal of what Olaf was surprised to discover was a German U-boat. It was a remnant from World War II.

The digging continued over the next two days, with more workers cycling in and out of the site. By the third day, the structure was almost completely removed from the ice. Dennis, the multinational head of the company, had only just arrived. He stepped to the edge of the ice, beyond which the U-boat pointed crooked out of the ice.

"This is truly impressive. When did you guys find it?", "Two days ago," answered another man, Knut—the regional manager. "One of our guys was out to perform some tests beneath the ice, and the probe smashed against it. Eight meters beneath the surface."

"Do the police know about the discovery? Or the local government?"; "Not yet. Anything we find here is technically yours, so we thought it might be better to get your input on it first.", Dennis nodded thoughtfully. "How about the internals? Anyone manage to get in yet?", "Not yet. We're trying to force open the hatch on the conning tower, but it's stuck. It could be any number of things keeping it sealed.", "Not surprising."

"But we did also figure the boat's pretty beat up. If it was sunk in battle, there should already be a few openings we can go through once it's all thawed out.", "What about identification? Any visible credentials?", "Not that I noticed.", "Isn't that strange, that a military vehicle has no immediate identification on its conning tower."

"Well now that you mention it, that is strange.", Dennis inhaled to ask yet another question when his phone began to audibly vibrate. "Excuse me," he said, lifting a finger to Knut. He pulled the phone from his pocket, checked the caller ID, and answered. "Hey, Butch…yes. Yes, I'm there now. You're not going to believe—", *"Anda logo!"* somebody screamed aloud, Dennis looked up from his phone. People were moving quickly towards the boat, *"Anda logo!"* they were keeping yelling; "What are they saying?" Dennis asked Knut; "They're saying to hurry."

Dennis raised the phone back to his head. "You know what, Butch? I'm going to have to call you back. I think we've just found something *huge*."

CHAPTER V

SOMEWHERE IN NORTHERN ATLANTIC OCEAN

It seemed like they'd been aboard the ship for an eternity. The Portuguese had made the trip fairly pleasant. The food was standard naval fare—the beds too—and the bathroom had been surprisingly clean. All that aside, Cristoph still fumed every day until the last, when the captain finally came knocking on their door to announce that they'd reached their destination.

The captain came in with four other officers and his translator. Apparently, they'd rehearsed the speech beforehand because the translator jumped right in without a prompt from his superior: "We've arrived at Cape Verde. These men are going to blindfold you, and you will be escorted to the rafts. They will take you ashore.", "This is absurd," Cristoph scoffed. "We're being treated as criminals."; "If you cannot see each other, you cannot cause any trouble." That was all the explanation Daniel and Cristoph were given. Though it wasn't enough for Cristoph, Daniel understood the necessity. It was he who first stepped forward and allowed himself to be blindfolded. Seeing that it was useless to offer any other objections, Cristoph too submitted to the plan.

Outside the room was noticeably warmer. The ship's hallway was stuffed with sweaty sailors, some of whom had apparently refused to shower. A rank odor permeated through the air and carried along the length of the hallway.

A line of Portuguese soldiers stood shoulder to shoulder in the hallway, forming a barricade of sorts as well as a means to effectively lead the men towards the lifeboats. Daniel felt body heat pressing against his back, hot and sticky.

"Why pack us so tight?" Daniel gasped in is mother tongue, "We're not cattle.", Cristoph responded with a sharp nudge and shushed Daniel; "But—" Before the words could come out, Cristoph nudged him again, harder, and said "no" in English so plain and perfect that it caught Daniel off guard. But a moment later, he realized why it was that Cristoph wanted him quiet. They had no idea with whom they were being herded.

"What's that I smell?" A man behind him asked in a condescending tone. "Filthy wankers all smell the same.", "Oi," another British man added. "Dishonor has that distinctive smell, don't it?", "Bloody well does."; Daniel heard Cristoph growl next to him.

"You put a lotta my friends under," the first Brit shouted. "What do you say I return the favor?", "You're welcome to try," Cristoph shouted back in thick German and edged backward to find his antagonist. But all he found was the freshly pressed shirt of a Portuguese sailor. They'd disseminated into the ranks of their captives to prevent just that kind of conflict.

At the front of the line, the interpreter called for them to all calm down. He reminded them all that it was a miracle any of them survived at all and advised they not waste the opportunity to arrive safely in their homelands. The call of home was enough to placate the lot of them. As for Daniel, the warning only served to remind him again how much the war had taken from him. Up to that very moment, his family remained in the dark regarding his whereabouts. The Portuguese were his only chance at getting a message to them, if Cristoph didn't stand in his way. To that end, he refused to take the bait of any disgruntled sailors among them. Germany had taken as much from him as it had from them. He knew it was wrong to pity the enemy or to sympathize with them, but he also knew what was most important to him and it wasn't the war: they eventually reached the lifeboats that would take them ashore. The interpreter divided them up into smaller groups, taking special care to keep the British and Germans separated. Daniel wasn't sure who they ended up with. Their lifeboat smelled like fresh plastic. It was cold and only grew more so the longer they remained on it. From what Daniel could hear, a good number of Portuguese sailors accompanied them. The other survivors packed in with them didn't speak a single word on the trip to shore. Daniel preferred it that way. The less conflict, the better.

In short time, they reached the shore. The Portuguese

shepherded them off and further separated the groups. They were quickly loaded into the back of a cargo truck and given no indication of where they were headed. The doors were closed behind them, shuttering out all the light, except for a faint ray through a small hole in the corner of the cargo box. Even Cristoph, who had been civilly disobedient until then, sat silently against the wall. He mumbled occasionally about unfairness and international law, but otherwise kept to himself.

Daniel knew it was best not to bother him, so he fiddled with his fingers until the truck came to its final stop. The front doors could be heard opening, then footsteps increasing gradually in volume, and then the back door finally opened. Light filtered through, temporarily blinding the two; One of the soldiers spoke in Portuguese and motioned with his arms for the men to exit. They did as instructed. Each of them was lead into a building—this was evident by both the smell and coolness of the air. They moved straight only a short distance, took several turns, and finally came to another room. The temperature in there was a bit warmer though it smelled less pleasant.

Someone said something in Portuguese. Soon after, their blindfolds were removed. Both were surprised to find they were in another holding area. Like their quarters in the ship, this one came complete with beds. Daniel smiled at this revelation. Cristoph did not. The doors closed behind them. Again, they were left in the dark.

Cristoph's first impulse was to escape. Of course, the door

was locked from the outside, but that was but a minor obstacle to him. He banged on the door and shouted until his voice went hoarse. Being who he was, that only made him bang harder. Daniel backed off and made himself comfortable on the bed. He saw no reason to abuse the hospitality of their benefactors. He watched from his seat as Cristoph beat his fists raw against the door. If anyone had been stationed outside their door, they waited until the only sound coming from the room was Cristoph's heavy panting before opening the door and stepping in.

"I demand to speak with a commanding officer," Cristoph gasped, "Here. You wait." The guard spoke with a thick Portuguese accent. Evidently, his understanding of the language was rudimentary at best though good enough that the parties could effectively communicate; "What gives you the right to hold us here? We've broken no laws and are entitled to contact our countrymen."; "This not Naziland. You no power. Stay here." The guard left no further room for debate. The door quickly closed, trapping the two once more without any idea when they'd be able to return home.

Cristoph cursed in German. "This is ridiculous! I'm a colonel—a goddamn colonel in the army—and denied my rights." He turned and punched the door and screamed, then panted and paced to the back wall.

"Please calm down.", "*Deutsch!*" Cristoph yelled across the room.

Daniel gulped and did as he was told. "At least we're on

land now. We're closer to home than we were on their ship.", "What good does that do if we can't contact command? We need to let them know we survived. Or has your fondness for a warm bed completely stripped you of the memory that we are on a mission?"

"No, but—look, if we want to get out, we need to be on their good side. We can't yell our way to a communication line. Portugal may be neutral, but we're the ones they sympathize with, right?", "That's right.", "Maybe we can use that to our advantage.", "Maybe." Cristoph's breathing slowed. "But we are still their prisoners.", that sentiment did not linger long, because the door opened shortly after. A different man entered.

"Good morning gentlemen," he said with a smile. "I am Colonel Salgado." He raised a brow at Cristoph. "I hear you've been requesting to speak with an officer? I am the highest ranked officer stationed here. May I know your names and ranks?"

"I am Colonel Zeigler of the German Army. My companion is a seaman of the same unit. As for that unit, we are not authorized to disclose its details. That said, I formally request to contact the German Embassy or my High Command, whichever suits you."

The Portuguese colonel considered the request for a moment. "Very well. I will put you in contact with your command."

Daniel saw his opportunity there. Even if he suffered the repercussions, the both of them were at the mercy of the

Portuguese. Whatever decision they came to would supersede Cristoph's antiquated understanding of soldiery; and Daniel counted on it being significantly more sympathetic. He stepped forward: "May I also be put in contact with my family through the German embassy?", "Not now." Cristoph's voice was sharp like a knife cutting through air. Even the Portuguese colonel flinched at its sound. "Remember we are soldiers at war. Our mission depends upon the same secrecy that forces us to so rudely withhold our unit from our benefactors." That last word was even sharper than the rest. Daniel felt it dig into his ears and puncture his conscience. "But sir, I—", "I know your family is important to you, soldier, but the Reich comes first. This is an order: you will not contact your family."

Daniel held in his retort. He swiveled his head over to the Portuguese colonel. He was nodding gravely. It made sense. Even in captivity, Cristoph was his superior. Officers of other nations would respect their chain of command. "Yes, sir," he muttered, doing his best to mask the disdain in his voice.

"I'll return shortly," the Portuguese colonel said and exited. Both men waited patiently for him to return, and when he did, Cristoph was visibly pleased. The colonel entered with a radio and his translator, and he shut the door behind him. "I have managed to get in contact with the Navy Attaché to the German Embassy stationed in Lisbon."

"Excellent." Cristoph was quick to take possession of the radio. He spoke quickly and with as much sophistication as possible to throw off the interpreter, whose presence there seemed an affront to the charity of the Portuguese. "This is Colonel Zeigler. I am currently being detained by the Portuguese and request that you immediately put me through to General Von Kleist."

"Good evening," said the voice on the other side of the radio. "Now, Colonel, I have been made aware of your situation. However, I have been unable to find your name among those listed as MIA. Could you please give me your unit?"

Cristoph scoffed off the radio, then clicked the button. "I am not authorized to disclose that information, but you may rest assured that the general can vouch for me."

"You must know the policy, Colonel. This is procedure. If you cannot verify your identity, I'll have to dismiss this communication."

"What's your name, son?" Cristoph's face grew increasingly red. His fist clenched and he began pacing around the room again.

"You must also know that I cannot disclose that until you can properly identify yourself. I need to know that you really are one of ours. Now I'll ask you one more time: what is your unit, Colonel?"

That's when Cristoph lost it. He banged the radio against the bed. Then in an unprecedented show of anger, howled into the radio. "I serve the same army as you! We fight for the same country! Now put me through to Von Kleist!" His chest lifted heavily as he awaited the response. There was a silence on the other end like the radio operator was deliberating his response.

Daniel took that as his moment. Cristoph was distracted. He moved forward quickly and grabbed the radio from his superior. "This is seaman Daniel Sommer. Can you please tell my family I'm safe?"

Cristoph reached for the phone, but Daniel was too quick. He maneuvered around the bed as the operator responded, "Sommer? S-O-M-M-E-R?", "That's correct," Daniel gasped. Cristoph backed him into a corner. The colonel's full weight came upon him like as wave at sea.

The radio was wrenched from his hands. It felt with a thud against the door. Cristoph looked down at it, enraged. His anger all recoiled against Daniel with a heavy shove that sent him sprawling against the bed.

"Don't you ever go over my head! Never again, Sommer!", at the door, the colonel gave his interpreter a quizzical expression. The interpreter went immediately to work explaining what had transpired in the conversation. Cristoph's unwillingness to cooperate with his own people and Daniel's frantic plea to contact his family demonstrated that something was amiss with the two men. Hearing the story, the colonel's expression changed from understanding to unamused.

"The both of you will remain confined in this room until we learn your true identities. At that time, we will decide what to do with you.", "I've already given you my name and rank."

"Which is why it is strange that you would not extend the same courtesy to your own countrymen who, may I remind you, *you* begged *me* to get into contact with. Worse still, they found no record of your in their enlistments. How do you expect me to interpret this?", "You think we're spies?" Cristoph stammered, "It's like I said, we will discover who you are ourselves. This exchange has proven one thing to me. You cannot be trusted."

The Portuguese colonel left in a hurry with his translator scurrying behind. The lock clicked from the other side; Daniel buried his face in the sheets and cursed his poor fortune.

CHAPTER VI

ST. TROPEZ, PROVENCE-ALPES-CÔTE D'AZUR, FRANCE

Minor clouds blocked off just enough sun that it was neither sweltering nor too cold for George to enjoy sunbathing on his yacht. After three years of keeping himself mostly holed up in his office and rarely ever going home, he'd finally caught just the break he needed to wind down from everything. It was all about hiring people who could work together to stand in for him in moments like that. If nothing else, he did an excellent job of choosing those individuals.

George rolled over and closed his eyes. The sun glowed red against his lids. His back trembled lightly. It was odd since the waves had been mostly calm that day. He hoped a storm wasn't on the horizon.

His back trembled again. Of course, it wasn't storm It was his phone. George answered without even bothering to check the caller, "What is it?"

"Hey, Boss, something came up in the office that I think you're going to want to see."

"Why? I'm on vacation. The reason you're there is to take care of that business while I'm gone. For Christ's sake, what is it that you idiots can't handle yourselves?"

"George, you know I wouldn't call if this wasn't big."

That much was true. Butch was a good worker, one of the best. But still, cutting into his vacation time was unacceptable. George grunted. "Explain. Now."

"I don't know if I—"

"Well if you want me over there, you damn well better try."

"Look, Boss, things are still developing on my end. It's hard to say for sure, but it's also pretty clear that this is *huge*."

George mumbled indistinctly to himself. He'd known Butch a long time, long enough to trust his judgment. Hell, he trusted Butch enough to give him extended authority during his vacation. He grunted again, this time so Butch could hear him.

"I'll come out there, but this better be as big as you say.",

"That's going to be the least of your worries once you get here."

George hung up the phone after that. He sat and relished in the sunlight for a few minutes more. Then he picked up his phone again. His next call was to his pilot to prep his jet for an impromptu trip to New York.

CHAPTER VII

SANTIAGO ISLAND, CAPE VERDE

Daniel watched from the comfort of his bed. It was the only luxury he had and one he intended to take full advantage of. He still had no word on the safety of his family, so it was the best he could do to assume they remained unaware of his present situation. The thought troubled him day in and day out. Nonetheless, he refused to let it kill what remained of his spirits.

Cristoph on the other hand spent more time pacing around the room than he did sleeping. It was true that Daniel also found getting a good night's sleep difficult, but when he couldn't get back to sleep, he merely lay there content with his thoughts. Cristoph took to the floor instead, raving on about the injustices they were suffering yet doing nothing to help alleviate the situation.

What could be done though? The two of them were at the whims of the Portuguese.

"Three days!" Cristoph barked. "We've been here three days and all we get is the occasional meal. Corroborating our stories my ass. They only want to keep us quiet."

"We didn't tell them anything," Daniel whispered from bed. Cristoph still fumed over the fiasco with the radio. Since then, Daniel did everything in his power not to upset his superior officer. That meant chiming in only when necessary and making sure he wasn't a detriment to their morale.

"*I* surely didn't. And it should remain that way, that we don't.", "You're right." Daniel gulped. "I was wrong. I shouldn't have taken the radio. I'm nervous and scared.", "And you have sworn fealty to the Third Reich and Fuhrer. Remember that." - "I remember." Daniel's voice came out smaller than a whisper. He assumed the role of the sycophant. If that's what it took to keep him alive, he intended on playing that role well., "Good." Cristoph stopped pacing and smiled for the first time in three days. "I'll see to it that I get us out of here."

It was no sooner than Cristoph made this vow that the door to their room opened and the Portuguese Colonel entered with his interpreter. He took a deep breath and began.

"I apologize for earlier, Colonel, but you must understand that maintaining strict policy is what keeps our countries afloat so to speak.", with a pleased smile stretched across his face, Cristoph stepped forward to shake the man's hand. "Again, I am Colonel Zeigler of the German army."

"Well, Colonel, I've been able to confirm the accuracy of your story. General Von Kleist would be pleased to speak with you. However, he made one condition: he'll speak to you and only you."

"I'll take him now if he's available." Cristoph puffed out his chest.

"Actually, the general will be coming here. Well, not here per se. He's scheduled to arrive in Lisbon and you are to meet him there tomorrow at noon."

On that note, the duo left the room. Daniel hadn't believed for a second that their presence there would be acknowledged by German high command. After all, everything else was shrouded in secrets. But he had no complaints. Even if he wasn't to tag along for the meeting, he felt himself getting significantly closer to a reunion with his family.

CHAPTER VIII

DOWNTOWN MANHATTAN, NEW YORK CITY

The office was exactly as George had left it. He slumped in his chair, looking disinterestedly at the financial analysis glowing on his computer screen. He should have still been on vacation soaking up rays from the sun not radiation from his computer.

Butch had made a big deal about whatever was going on, enough that George felt adequately convinced that he needed to return, but he also had the expectation that he'd be swamped with news. Alas, his office was empty and quiet. He'd already tried contacting Butch twice that day. Both times, the call went directly to voicemail. Another nail in the coffin.

George sat for a long half-hour before the intercom finally buzzed and the voice of his assistant came through.

"George? Butch just called to let you know he'll be here in a few hours."

George slumped further down in his seat. They hadn't actually arranged for a specific time to meet. George knew for that reason alone, he couldn't be entirely frustrated. It was the anxiety that was really getting to him, the need to know exactly what mandated he put a hasty end to his vacation.

There was no use sulking about it. As long as he was back and had time to kill, George figured he might as well get something done. For those two hours, he went over the financial reports. Time slipped swiftly away as he worked. Soon enough, the door opened. Butch came in. He wasn't alone either. With him was Dennis and someone else—a girl he didn't recognize; "Who is this?" he asked, rising from his seat, "Emily Wood. We hired her as a consultant on this matter."

George quickly stole a glance at the finances spreadsheet. "What matter? Let's get to the heart of the issue.", "Emily?" Butch motioned the girl forward. She cleared her throat nervously.

"Three days ago, a group of operators in Greenland found a boat buried in the ice."

"Alright, so someone sunk their boat. Why does that require me to be here?"

"Because the boat was German in origin. It's a U-boat from World War Two."

George placed cupped his chin and looked up in thought. "Butch? You really couldn't handle this yourself?"

"I did, Boss. We uncovered it and cracked it open and…and the crew was still there."

Emily jumped in to finish: "But that's not even the most interesting part. I study this kind of thing so I know that typically a boat of that size would be manned by about fifty people. There were only twenty aboard. And yes, I know that some might have escaped when the boat sunk, but that doesn't explain the internal structure. It's been expressly modified to be manned by a smaller crew. Not only that but all of the weapons storage areas had been cleared out, replaced with batteries and fuel.", "Okay, and what exactly does that mean?"

Dennis chimed in now with his own enthusiastic explanation. "We have absolutely no idea. Even the sonar and navigational equipment had been tampered with if not downright removed."

"It was wartime," George sighed. "It makes sense that they might not want to be discovered. The element of surprise."

"That's true", Emily said, "but then why not develop a boat specifically for that purpose?"

"Exactly", Dennis chimed in. "There were huge empty compartments in there. That boat was transporting something huge and the Germans didn't want anyone to know about it; And this boat has fallen right into our hands"

George was beginning to see the magnificence of it. It wasn't just a relic from a time long past. The discovery of the boat, if all their hypothesizing was correct, marked a monumental discovery. "Who else knows about it?"

Butch cleared his throat: "Only the small group that discovered it. They're at work reburying it for now. Not even the local authorities know yet."

"Good. So which one of you wants to tell me exactly what you think it is this submarine was carrying?"

Emily spoke. "Several reports indicate that the Nazis were

consolidating their gold near the end of the war. I think this U-boat might have been one of the transport vehicles. It was probably en route to a covert base before it sunk."

"Yeah," Dennis added. "And still there's more to the story. See, there's a hole in the boat's hull similar to what you might expect from a collision with an iceberg. Chances are, with the reduced crew, they didn't have enough people to look out for that kind of thing. And without any navigational equipment, the had no chance in hell. Now, a good bit of the inside is scorched to hell. We're guessing once they knew they were going to sink, they torched the place themselves. We couldn't find anything to identify the boat except for a swastika and a lockbox full of documents. It's a sturdy box, even by modern standards. Survived being submerged for so long. And does anyone want to guess what we found in it?" He didn't wait for anyone to answer. "Official documents pertaining to the explicit details of the mission. The only problem is that most of the pages are badly damaged. The lockbox couldn't keep all the water out, but there's a page on the top that was slightly legible. The letters *DDE* were written across it."

"We think it stands for *Die Deutche Eigentum*, which translates to 'German property', There's a chance that the gold is still out there. Given all the space onboard that we're presuming was reserved for the gold, the Germans probably assumed the ship sunk irretrievably when the boat didn't check in. But look, that gold has to be somewhere. I did the math based on the cargo space and we're looking at 200 tons."

George raised an eyebrow, "That's roughly eight billion dollars," Butch explained.

George rose from his seat. A vein bulged in his forehead. A eight billion dollar find off the coast of Greenland and it just happened to fall into his company's hands. No doubt if anyone else got wind of it, they'd be able to piece together the same story that Emily did. And most likely, the local government would assume ownership. Before that happened, he needed to retrieve the cargo.

"Have you swept the surrounding area for it? There has to be some way to get a general sweep of—"

Butch interrupted him abruptly: "George, you're going to want to sit down. You too, Emily. The report's not quite over yet, but don't you worry about finding it. Dennis and I actually already have something in mind."

CHAPTER IX

SANTIAGO ISLAND, CAPE VERDE

The days following the announcement that German high command would be acknowledging Daniel and Cristoph were wrought with an air of happiness neither man had felt since the sinking of their ship. Daniel especially wore a wide smile. He'd finally be getting a chance to return to his family. He was reasonably nervous though considering his outburst may have caused some tension for those within the upper echelons of German high command who were aware of the secret mission.

Daniel looked over to Cristoph who was in deep contemplation and called out to him: "How much longer do you think it'll take for this meeting?"

Cristoph shook his head. "I don't know. We are cut off from our allies. There is no telling what is going on outside this room."

Daniel replied: "We should have been placed on a missing persons list when our boat sank. I have a bad feeling about this pickup taking so long."

"Oh boy," Cristoph scoffed. "I'm sorry, Daniel. Because

of the nature of this mission, I haven't been able to tell you much, but maybe you deserve to know this much: the boat we were on was much more than an undetectable submarine. And our mission was far more important than remaining unseen."

"What's that supposed to mean?" Daniel raised an eyebrow. He was familiar with the tone Cristoph fell into. He was emphatically stopping every few words to gauge Daniel's reaction. That meant he would only talk for as long as he felt the truth wasn't too much for Daniel to handle. Realizing this, Daniel steeled himself against surprise.

"It means that certain measures were in place.", "Measures like what? I gave them my name. All they had to do was cross-reference it with the list of MIA soldiers to verify our situation."

"Actually, that wouldn't have verified anything. As far as any radio operator is concerned, everyone who was on that boat died a long time ago."

Daniel did his best to hide the fear in his voice. "What does that mean?"; "Daniel…" Cristoph sighed. "In the few days following our departure, the families of all the crew were alerted that all onboard personnel were killed in an air raid."

There was a silence while Daniel processed what he'd just been told. His family wasn't waiting home for him? They were mourning his loss, thinking he'd never return? He thought of the funeral they must have had without a body to attach to the reality and all the tears they must have shed. Daniel clenched his fists.

"Sommer, please understand, we—"; "You've been letting me believe I had something to go home to.", "I've been trying to get you to stop believing in it ever since we took you on. But you need to understand, we did it because we needed to. It was vital to the secrecy of the mission that the crew on that submarine didn't officially exist".

"You son of a bitch!" Daniel charged forward without restraint, pinning Cristoph to the nearest wall. "You know how much this has meant to me." He thought about raising a fist and beating his commanding officer to a pulp, but he couldn't; "Go ahead," Cristoph egged. "Get it all out."

Daniel fumed at the mouth. His breathing was completely out of control, erratic. He huffed and considered his options. If he hurt Cristoph in any way, his chances of seeing his family were that much smaller. Or maybe it didn't have to be that way. Maybe with Cristoph out of the picture, he'd actually be closer. But what it a risk he was willing to take? Absolutely not. Daniel backed off.

Seemingly unfazed by the event, Cristoph straightened up his clothes and returned to his pacing. "It was not my decision to make.", "That's not an excuse," Daniel shot back; "But I did it for my country, as should you."

"I never wanted to be a part of this!" Daniel almost got it in him to push Cristoph back against the wall, but the door opened. Both of them turned quickly to see who had entered.

It was Salgado and his translator. The former carried a radio, "General Von Kleist is currently prepared to speak with you," the translator said.

Cristoph was quick to snatch up the radio. He clacked his heels together and raised his arm in a formal salute. "Hail Hitler, General." Daniel narrowed his eyes at Cristoph, always so needlessly formal, so completely driven by his allegiance to Germany. They all learned the procedures in military academy, but it went beyond patriotism to salute someone through a radio.

"Fucking idiot," Daniel muttered. It's not as though Cristoph was wearing the military-issue boots that made the distinctive smash when the heels touched. It didn't make any sense. Daniel doubted his countrymen more and more every day. These were people who would destroy the families of those who fought for them if it meant they could push their soldiers a little bit further.

"Hail Hitler," Von Kleist parroted. "It is a pleasure to hear from you again.", "Likewise. It is my understanding that you plan on retrieving us from the Portuguese?"; "I will send General Weber for this matter. You are to trust him as though were me. That's an order. Am I clear?", "Yes, sir!", "You are to report the status of the mission to Weber in person. Once you've reached the mainland and contact the Lisbon embassy, I'll arrange for a meeting with you. I'm currently en route to that location.", "It will be good to stand among my brothers and sisters once more, General."; "Doubtlessly. Now…is Daniel Sommer with you now? I'd like to speak with him."

Cristoph looked quizzically at Daniel. To his knowledge,

General Von Kleist had no reason to want to speak with Daniel. Daniel, too, felt the same and it showed on his face. Simultaneously, they both harbored the thought that Daniel's outburst from earlier had reached high command and they were about to understand the repercussions of that action. Cristoph apprehensively handed the radio over to Daniel.

"This is Seaman Sommer.", "The Reich will not forget what you have sacrificed, son."; Daniel gulped: "Thank you, sir."

"I would like you to know that your wife and son are perfectly safe. The war has brought no harm to them. I share this information with you in confidence."

Daniel began to tear up. He had no way to know for certain if the General was telling the trust. Amidst all the lies the Germans had already fed him, it was a colossal task to separate the truth from the lies, but something in his voice sounded torn, as though he wasn't only apologizing to Daniel but to himself as well.

"And as proof of my sincerity, I have prepared a surprise for you today.", Daniel brought the radio closer to his ear and listened carefully.

"Daddy?"

He could hardly believe what he was hearing. "Franz? Is that you?", the kid's voice sounded trough the radio loud and clear: "I'm so happy I get to talk to you.", "Me too, Franz." The tears grew into each other. Daniel's hands trembled; the radio shook in them. But at the same time, he had to wonder—he couldn't let his joy overshadow his rationality—why Franz didn't think he was dead. "Franz? Can you tell me where Mom is? Can you put her on for me?"

"Your friends came to pick me up from school. They took me to talk with you. They told Mom to go home."

Daniel's eyes widened. "Was she okay when you saw her?", "Yes but she said you wouldn't be home for a long time, Dad. Is that true?"

Daniel fought to keep a strong face up for his son, knowing all the while that the German army had him in a voice grip. "I don't know. I'll try to come home as soon as I can, okay?"

"Okay. Why haven't you written back to me while you've been gone? I miss you."

That was the final nail. Either his wife had kept the letters to herself after learning falsely that Daniel was dead or the Germans were cutting off communication between the two. Either way, it broke Daniel to learn that his son had shown such unrewarded dedication.

"I'm sorry, Franz. I don't think any of your letters made it to me. I've been at sea, so maybe that's why." It was the best excuse he could think of on his feet.

"I hope you can read them soon! Did you find the book I wanted? The one with the girl who jumps in the hole?"

It was something Daniel had all but forgotten. Franz had wanted a copy of *Alice in Wonderland* for months. Daniel promised that when he came home, he'd bring a copy of the book with him: "I haven't forgotten. I'll bring it to you."

"They told me you'll be here in two days. I can't wait to see you. I wish Mom could be here too."

Daniel's fist clenched. *Damn Nazis, targeting my son. Cowardly bastards.* But more importantly, if his wife was safe … "Why won't your mom be there?", "They said she was coming to pick you up so we have to see you separately".

Daniel didn't believe them. Not one bit. But he pretended like it was a detail he'd forgotten. "That's right! Yes, she will be coming. I need you to be strong for now, okay? Do what my friends ask of you."

"I will," Franz laughed. He was so happy and oblivious to everything happening around him. It only stoked Daniel's anger to know his son got caught between himself and the people who entrapped him on the secret mission.

There was some shuffling around on the radio, then the General returned to speak: "I need you to continue fighting this war, Seaman. You are in a very significant position although you may not realize it now. What I need from you is for you to follow the instruction of you commanding officer. If he needs your silence, be silent. If he needs your rashness, be rash. If he needs your sacrifice, do not hesitate to sacrifice. Do this, and your family will see you again. Disobey and you will not return home."

"Y-yes sir." *Was that a threat?* Daniel thought. If the mission was so important that Daniel would be killed by his own people for failure to comply, why couldn't they at least tell him what it was? Von Kleist ended the communication before Daniel had a chance to ask any of his burning questions.

The Portuguese translator had been busy recounting the details of the radio transmission to his superior who was nodding solemnly. He looked at Daniel once with beady eyes and once at Cristoph with suspicion, but he overall seemed to have objectively absorbed the information.

The translator conveyed the message: "It's a pleasure to hear that your rescue has been sorted out, Colonel.", Cristoph replied: "Thank you. We are indebted to your kindness and patience.", "We will keep in contact with the German embassy and provide and updates that might be relevant to you. When the general arrives to collect you, you will be sent for. We expect he should arrive within the next twenty-four hours, but as you know, things don't always go as planned." Cristoph thanked the Portuguese Colonel again.

"I don't know who the two of you *really* are or what your mission, but the secrecy of this must mean you have a very important role to play. I pray you both survived it."

On that note, Salgado left the room. It grew cold and quiet. After the radio conversation, Cristoph seemed put off.

Nothing pleased the man. Daniel was glad to hear that they wouldn't be stranded indefinitely with the Portuguese. There was finally another occasion to smile. After all the fuss he made about getting in contact with German high command, it was strange that Cristoph should be so disconcerted. Daniel didn't need to ask why though. Cristoph jumped straight into the heart of the matter.

"Are you sure that you spoke with your son?" he said with a quite concerned sound in his voice; "How dare you even— you think I don't know the voice of my own son? First you tore him away from me, then from his mother. How far does this need to go? I swear to you, I—" Cristoph raised a hand; "As I've explained before, those decisions were not up to me. I wouldn't have sanctioned something so boorish. But I need you to forget about your emotions and think for me. Are you absolutely sure that was your son?"

The fact that Cristoph didn't sign off on the kidnapping only brought him a slight peace of mind. "You think I wouldn't recognize the voice of my own son? How else could he know I was supposed to bring him a book? We had that conversation in private only days before I left.", "What was the book, Daniel?", "It was *Alice in Wonderland*. He's wanted to read it for months." "Could he have told your wife?", "He wouldn't have. It was a secret between us. She loves to read him stories before bed, so it was as much a surprise for her as it was for him. Why would you even doubt it was my son? I haven't been told anything about this mission and it's beyond annoying now."

"Because." Cristoph took a deep breath. "That was not General Von Kleist." "What do you mean? We've heard his voice a million times in speeches and on the radio. There's no mistaking it.", "No, there's not, but we had a very specific plan in place for moments like this. He told us where, when, and to whom we should report.", "And what's wrong with that?"

"I never asked. The plan had always been for me to ask if I should immediately report. He was supposed to decline that offer and suggest instead that we be debriefed in person. Moreover, we weren't supposed to meet with the General in person.", "But that's what he did." "He shall have said that sentence after me asking to report, I was about to do that but he preceded me.", "Those are small details, Cristoph. They probably don't mean anything.", "If you know General Von Kleist at all, you should know that he *never* steers away from a plan, even if it means running headfirst towards his death. There's no denying it. That was not him."

Typical Nazi paranoia. Always the secrecy with them. It was no wonder they struggled with trusting anything. If Cristoph was right, something sinister was in the works. There would be no telling whether or not his family was alive. And if Cristoph was wrong, he'd soon be able to see his family.

But Cristoph couldn't have been right. With as many speeches as the General had delivered, he would be hard-pressed to doubt himself regarding his authenticity. And as for his own son's voice. He still fumed at the accusation that he wouldn't immediately recognize little Franz. Still, Cristoph had said enough to instill some doubt in him. Only time would tell the truth.

CHAPTER X

SANTIAGO ISLAND, CAPE VERDE

Twenty-four hours passed with the two men running circles in their minds. What was true and what was false? After the radio contact and they were left alone, Daniel argued relentlessly with Cristoph about how they should interpret what just happened. Cristoph, who was immensely more informed of the mission logistics, eventually won out that battle. It was only reluctantly that Daniel admitted it was in his best interest to follow Cristoph's judgment as much as he hoped it was wrong.

"What would they gain by lying to us?" Daniel demanded, Cristoph had no answer except, "Secrecy."; That wasn't enough to satisfy Daniel. He was happy though that his comrade now knew what it felt like to be blatantly lied to by his superiors and kept in the dark while his life hung in the balance. The Nazi lies did no good for anyone involved.

Well into the evening that day, Salgado returned to the room with good news. "General Weber is here," he announced through his translator. "and he is waiting for the two of you.", Cristoph raised an eyebrow. "He wants to see both of us? I thought Daniel was to stay behind for this meeting."

"It seems that things have changed," Salgado explained.

It felt bittersweet finally getting to leave the room. Although they'd walked down the same hallway the day they arrived, it seemed much different to Daniel now. It smelled fresher than their quarters ever had and, although it certainly was not, the hallway seemed better lit. Cristoph walked ahead of Daniel and held his hand to his chin the whole time; He had a terrible habit of getting caught up in little details. Maybe plans changed and there simply wasn't a good direct line of communication to convey those changes to two soldiers lost at sea.

As for Daniel, he awaited the closure of finally verifying when he'd get to see his son again; They arrived at the end of the corridor, moved through several other hallways, and ultimately reach an open door on the other side of which was a cozy room. But standing in front of that pathway were two German soldiers and General Weber. The general stood with his hands on his hips, drawing attention to the gun on his waist.

"Hail Hitler!" Cristoph said nervously, "Hail Hitler!" the general responded. "It is a pleasure to finally meet you, Colonel. Please." He motioned his arms and stepped aside. "After you.", Cristoph and Daniel both stepped forward, but Weber held out an arm to block Daniel.

"I thought you wanted to see us both, sir?", "These are private matters, sailor. You and Colonel Salgado will have to excuse us." The two soldiers remained outside of the room.

When Cristoph and Weber crossed the threshold, they pulled the door closed.

The soldier on the left sighed: "This must be some serious extraction. Thought we'd be in France right now, but high command plucked us out of the bunch."

Daniel looked surprised. The man bore a Westphalian accent. Daniel's hometown was in Westphalia. But why was this soldier disclosing that information so openly? High command knew his origin. Perhaps they were sent to test his allegiance somehow.

"If that's the case, I suppose we'll all be going back to the mainland together.", the solider on the right spoke up next. "Hopefully. Once your fellow finishes up with his report, we'll probably head straight back. By the way, you don't happen to be from Westphalia, do you?", "I am," Daniel answered, "Ah, I knew I couldn't be mistaking that accent. So we're all from the same place. If I'm lucky, they won't ship me off to Russia now that I know a little something about you."

Everyone laughed at that and Daniel relaxed. They seemed to be doing a better job coping with the secrecy of the mission than he was. At the very least, they gave the impression that they were not Nazi fanatics. Like him, they were merely soldiers following orders, completely cut off from the head of the German beast.

The left soldier spoke next. "Seriously, they didn't tell us nothing. We don't know who he is or the guy who was with you, neither we know anything about you; Apparently, you're both important, but they didn't even tell us that. We just figured you must be."

"There is much you don't know," Daniel said grimly. "The truth is, I'm Bavarian." He said this with a thick, comical accent. The three all laughed again. Tensions all dispersed and there was a moment of calm.

Unfortunately, that moment was short-lived. Screaming erupted from behind the closed door, escorts wouldn't recognize it, but Daniel knew it immediately as Cristoph's.

"No, you are not! I'm done with the bullshit!" Something—a table maybe—fell over in the room. It was followed by the sound of glass or porcelain shattering, and that was followed by even more screaming.

Among the three of them at the door, none was quite prepared to open the door and see what conflict the two officers inside had gotten into. The escorts slinked forward, eyeing one another apprehensively.

Daniel thought for a moment. As rash as Cristoph was, he could be in trouble. He doubted he himself could find himself in hot water if he intruded on the secret meeting for the sake of dispelling hostilities. Where the two escorts withdrew themselves from opening the door, Daniel moved forward with confidence, wrapping his hand around the knob.

The left soldier grabbed his hand. "Wait, Dan—", he stopped there. But it was too late. What could he possibly have been about to say besides Daniel's name? Which they just said they ignored? Danger? No, that wouldn't make any sense, not the way the tone in his voice had been.

Cristoph was right. Those men weren't who they claimed to be. Daniel pushed them both aside, then quickly opened the door. He found Cristoph there on the floor with blood pouring from a wound in his head. A quick pan to the left revealed the man who claimed to be General Weber laying a few meters away, also suffering from a head wound. A glass coffee table between them had somehow shattered. Glass had sprayed everywhere. But what latched most securely to Daniel's attention was Weber's gun a few feet from where Cristoph lay unconscious.

The two escorts rushed past Daniel, nearly knocking him to the ground in the process. They fell to their knees besides Weber and one of them—Daniel couldn't tell which—asked, "Are you okay?"

It rung as odd to Daniel. Not just the soldier's choice of words, but his tone as well. To speak to such a high ranking officer with such formality was unprecedented in the German military unless... *that was it*, in that moment, Daniel confirmed Cristoph's skepticism. His mind wandered from the present scene into a lengthy retrospective. Now he had no way of knowing the condition of his family. He could no longer say for sure whether or not he heard Franz's voice over the radio; and beyond that, he had no way of confirming whether or not his family was even alive. The thought sent a wave of terror from the soles of his feet to the hairs on his head. His heart pounded. If by some miracle Daniel still had a family to return to, they thought he was dead. They were either grieving or looking for a way to move on. Maybe they filled the void he left with someone else. Another wave of discomfort unsettled Daniel's bones.

"Who are you?" Daniel wondered aloud, eyes trained on the two escorts. They obviously weren't low-ranking soldiers. Without a doubt, they know more than he did. But that wasn't important. What *was* important was that Cristoph uncovered the truth which resulted in the altercation. Weber tried to kill him. And his gun was still there on the floor.

Even though Daniel was only a navigator, he had the weapons training necessary to make a confident dart for the gun. By the time anyone else in the room knew what was happening, he had scored the gun from the ground, released the safety, and pointed it straight for the General's head, blood rushed to his head. He'd never held a gun in a real combat situation, least of all pointed one at another human being. He felt the weight of the weapon in his hand. So much power in such a small package. Enough power to change the course of history. Where he stood, Daniel felt the gravity of the situation weigh down upon him.

"You are not allies!" Daniel barked across the room, the two men stared idly at him, "If any of you tries anything, I swear I'll shoot."

"Oh, I don't think that's going to happen." The voice was unfamiliar. It didn't come from either man—it couldn't have. It was the voice of an American, spoken in English. Daniel spun around to face the source of the voice. Standing beneath the threshold of the room's entrance was a casually-dressed man.

Daniel played with the possibility that the Americans had been screwing with them all along. Nazi reports indicated that they played dirty and would do anything to see the Reich fall, but subverting the authority of a neutral country just to kidnap and kill two officials. It didn't make sense. Nonetheless, Daniel didn't intend on giving them an opportunity to take advantage of his surprise. He turned the gun on the American.

"Take one more step into this room and I'll shoot you dead!", the American raised his hands in surrender. "No, Daniel, you won't.", "You really want to take that chance, American?", "Yes, actually." The man took a step forward, Daniel didn't hesitate. He closed his eyes and pulled the trigger… nothing happened.

"It's a model gun," the American explained. "No real firing mechanism.", "Lies!"; now the American started moving towards Daniel. Weber's attendants watched the scene wide-eyed, but neither of them dared to move. The gun misfired once but the chances of it misfiring twice weren't at all likely. Daniel already proved that he had the resolve to pull the trigger, and having crossed that boundary himself, subsequent squeezes of the trigger would come easier to him.

Daniel checked the gun over. He ejected the magazine. Real bullets. He emptied the chamber and cocked the weapon back. The American was only feet away now. Daniel aimed the gun at his forehead. The American halted.

"Not another step," Daniel warned, the American swayed forward, another click from the gun. Daniel squeezed the trigger again and again. Each time, it clicked. Now he was face to face with the American with nothing between them and no weapon to defend himself. Daniel stumbled backwards, tripping over Cristoph's outstretched leg. He tumbled awkwardly, then crawled backwards against the wall.

"Please," he sobbed. "I just want to see my family again. They think I'm dead—God—they think I'm dead.", "Don't worry," the American said. He reached into the breast pocket of his shirt. He pulled out a handkerchief. "Here, dry your eyes. No one will hurt you."

Daniel had no more room in his thoughts for doubt. He wanted the day to be over. He wanted the mission to be over. He wanted the war to be over. He wanted it all to be done with and for things to go back to the way they were before, when he was happy. Whatever the hell was going on, nobody deemed it necessary to clue him in. Maybe it was time for him to finally roll with the punches.

"Thank you." Daniel took the kerchief and dabbed his face with it. The American lowered down in front of him and placed a hand on his shoulder. The hand, like the cloth, was unusually soft. Americans were said to be technologically advanced. The handkerchief likely came out of one of their special factories. As for the man's hand, he heard nothing to suggest Americans had any warmth in their hearts at all. Despite that, there was a paternal aura spilling forth from the man.

"I know the things you've seen recently have been difficult to cope with. You probably want answers. If you trust me and cooperate, you just might get them.", surprisingly, negotiating terms with the American wasn't foremost of Daniel's mind. "I need a cigarette," he said between two deep breaths.

The American turned around and looked towards the door. There was someone else there, maybe even several people. It was impossible to know how many people were lurking nearby. The most immediately visible person was a woman. She was peeking apprehensively around the corner until the American man motioned to her. She came forward, pulled a box of Marlboros from her pocket, and pulled out a butte. Daniel leaned forward and clasped it between his lips. In her other hand, she already held a lighter. She clicked the flame to life. Daniel sucked in the flame and puffed.

He felt instantly better. Everything became a little clearer. The girl who'd lent him the cigarette was quite the looker. The American man was decent-looking as well. But now that he was calmed down, Daniel couldn't let himself be distracted by their appearances. Cristoph was still unconscious in the middle of the room. The Americans would take this opportunity to interrogate him. They'd want to know what kind of secret mission he and Cristoph were on and whether or not it had been successful. Daniel began to sweat all over again. He didn't even have the answers. How would they interpret his ignorance? As resistance, most likely. He'd be tortured. Yes, the Americans were ruthless. The niceties were a façade; they wouldn't hesitate to put him through the ringer.

"Thank you," Daniel said to the woman, trying not to sound too suspicious. Their eyes met for a while. Daniel didn't know whether or not he imagined it, but he thought he saw a flicker of embarrassment or anxiety there. He tried not to hold her gaze for too long.

"You're welcome," she responded in a thick British accent, *Shit,* Daniel thought. The Americans and the British were cooperating on this. Now there was no doubt in him mind that he'd be interrogated. "You're not American?" he asked her, drawing heavily from the cigarette and holding his head down so as not to let them see his fear; "No," she answered. "British."; "I was there for the British Empire Games a few years back.", the woman gave a puzzled expression, "Why are you looking at me like that?", "It's nothing. I just—"

The American raised a hand to silence her. The hierarchy was established, Daniel cleared his throat. "It's rude to run in here without introducing yourself. I take it you and your friends all already know me."

The America started talking straight: "Daniel Sommer, seaman. Born in Westphalia on February the third, 1905. Your son Franz was born twenty-three years later on March fifth. As for your wife, she—", "That's enough." It didn't surprise Daniel in the least that the American knew so much about him. He could have very well been pulling strings in the German high command. "I want to know who the hell you are.", "My name is George, I own an oil company, and I'm here to tell you what happened".

CHAPTER XI

SOMEWHERE IN GREENLAND
March, the 10th 2015

"You know what, Butch? I'm going to have to call you back. I think we've just found something *huge*." Dennis hung up the phone and stared out towards the gathering Norwegians. They moved quickly and in droves, gathering at a precise point in the ice. Knuth was already powering forward towards the mass of people. His limbs were unbelievably strong. Dennis could see it in Knuth's strut, even though he was twenty years Dennis's senior, that he didn't neglect taking care of his body. Dennis, on the other hand, escalated his breathing after striding only a few meters. "It's the cold weather," he told himself. Knuth was used to it, so of course he could move through it as though it was nothing. That made sense to Dennis.

Knuth kept several feet ahead of Dennis most of the way to the crowd. Once they'd cleared half of the distance, Dennis slowed down to take a better look at the crowd. They were frantic for sure, but it wasn't the kind of crazy hysteria he expected it to be. There was order to it. The people were all excited, straining to get a look at something on the inside of the structure.

They had to push through most of the bystanders to get anywhere relatively close to the front, and even when they did, the crowd had become so dense that it was impossible to move much further. Heads and limbs blocked off the structure from a clear view, but close to the front, Knuth pointed out a short man in a white shirt. He said something in Norwegian and the man turned around.

Dennis recognized him immediately. He'd scrutinized over dozens of headshots of doctors, and that man had been among them. Due to some legalese that he didn't quite understand himself, they were obligated to bring a doctor along during the excavation. George had been furious. Of course, they had to pay the doctor, and George saw it as a needless expense. He complained for days about how such an expense would never come in good use.

Knuth and the Norwegian doctor bean talking, presumably about whatever got the crowd so riled up. Even though he couldn't understand a word that was spoken between the two, it was clear by the expression on Knuth's face that he was in happy shock. He looked equal parts surprised and shocked and nervous. The longer the two spoke, the more those qualities rose to the surface of his expression and the more often he craned his head to get a good look into the U-boat. By the end of their dialogue, Knuth was in a state of utter disbelief. The doctor turned back around to explain something else to other officials on site. Knuth also turned around, to face Dennis,

"What was that about?" Dennis asked. "Why do you look so riled up?", "Follow me," Knuth said. He led Dennis around the crowd of people to an edge of the ice that was blocked off by crudely erected fencing and several guards. Both of the men flashed their IDs and were permitted beyond the gate, if only slightly. A few feet into the enclosure, another fence prohibited them from moving any deeper in. Knuth pointed.

Dennis didn't need the direction to know what he was supposed to be looking at. A man's face pressed against the edge of a block of ice just below the U-boat. He looked strained as though he was struggling to break himself out of the ice. Dennis couldn't imagine what kind of pain he must have been in during those last moments of his life.

"That doctor just now said they found him stuck in there. One of the guys who was chiseling the ice was actually the one to find him and he shone his flashlight and thought he might be imagining it, but he swore he saw the…the guy in the ice…and the doctor came to confirm it."

"Yeah, to confirm what? What did the doctor see?", "His pupils dilated."

CHAPTER XII

DOWNTOWN MANHATTAN, NEW YORK CITY
March, the 13th 2015

"Wait, wait, wait." George waved his hand dismissively. "You're telling me that you found one of the sailors and he was still alive? How is that even possible?"

Butch pursed his lips. Everyone had the same incredulous expression as George, and he couldn't blame them. He hardly believed it himself. "It would be better to say that he's only *technically* alive."

"What the hell is that supposed to mean?" George rose from his seat. His hands shook on the table. "Technically this, technically that. I don't want the technical details, Butch. Give it to me straight.", "When the submarine crashed into the iceberg, he was one of the sailors who fell overboard. Everyone wasn't so lucky, but he somehow got entrapped in the ice. We think he may be in a comatose state. Think of it as hibernation.", "You're shitting me".

Dennis blew out thoughtfully. "I wouldn't have believed it either if I hadn't seen it with my own eyes. His retina definitely reacted to changes in light. There's no way that'd be happening if he wasn't still alive in some capacity. What was it that the doctor said, Butch?"

"Besides being completely blown away by it, he went through all the bases with us. If the water and surrounding air are cool enough, and assuming you're close to, say, a hollowed out chunk of ice, it's not impossible for your body to enter a hibernation state before dying. He probably fell over close to where they struck the ice and got caught up in it."

"What are the chances?" George wiped his brow. "There's no way you can expect me to believe everything happened so perfectly."

"That's the thing, boss. None of us really believes it, even now. There's a one in a million chance that all the conditions are right. And even then, there are numerous other variables that could affect the outcome. We're talking about a miracle here, but that's exactly what happened."

George turned to Emily whose eyes were bulging out of their sockets. She held both hands over her mouth which would have otherwise been agape. "You didn't know about this either, did you?" George asked her.

She couldn't even gather her senses to respond. She shook her head slowly. George then turned to Dennis and Butch. He looked back and forth between the two, neither of which had anything further to say. They could see the fury in George's eyes and that he believed he was being lied to.

"Butch, I've known you a long time. I've trusted you. What have I done to make you entertain this ridiculous fantasy?", Then George sighed deeply. "You have never lied to me before so I'm going to assume that this is all true. I'm also going to assume that there's more to the story than what you've told me."

"You'd be right, boss. After we found the, uh, person, we thought it would be in our best interests to expand the search, so we looked at a radius of about 200 meters and...", "What is it? If you have anything worth saying, then say it!"

Dennis jumped in. "We found another sailor, frozen like the other. His retina dilated in response to light."

George slammed his hands on the desk. "You just told me there was a one in a million chance of this happening just *once*!"

"We also said there were a number of other variables," Butch defended. "Some of those variables would make it less likely, and others would make it more likely. Obviously they had to have fallen in at about the same time and near already-formed ice crystals. And—well, we think the fact that they were earing the exact same uniforms might have had something to do with it as well."

"What?" George gasped. "That's by far the most incredible thing I've heard in my whole life", Butch promptly replied: "I can easily believe that, boss, So do I".

"So who exactly are these men? Is there any way to identify them?", "Not as of now. None of them wore dog tags or patches. Whatever they were doing out there, it must have been a covert mission...which goes without saying, we weren't supposed to find them. No one was."; George rubbed his eyes slowly and thoughtfully. "Where are they now?", "Our Massachusetts facility under medical watch. We managed to get them thawed out, and they're surprisingly stable. For now, we have them under medically-induced comas."

"We can wake them then?" George looked excited for the first time since the group broke the news of the discovery to him, "Technically, yes.", "I'm done with it!" George started. "Enough with this technical shit. If you can't learn to speak anything other than this technical language, I don't have any use for you."; They were standing on one of the greatest discoveries of human history, and Butch was wasting time nitpicking at the smallest details, "There's a difference between—", "Fuck the technicality!" he said with a wave of his hand, "Okay, fine. Well here's where we are. Imagine if you went asleep tonight and woke up seventy-five years in the future. It would be traumatizing. We can wake them up, but if we do, there are certain measures we need to take to make sure they can properly adapt to waking up in a different time."; "Why is that a concern of mine?"

Emily jumped in. "Because I've been researching this submarine and the conditions of its demise, and I've yet to come up with anything about stripped-down U-boats on covert missions. This is my field of study. I'm confident that if anything even remotely related to this came up in history, I would have found a connection."

"I still fail to see why I should be concerned with that. When we wake them up, what use are these Nazi popsicles to me?", "It's true that Emily didn't know we'd found bodies, Boss, but we had her looking into the incident from the moment we discovered it. The historical part isn't finding humans preserved in ice, it's the circumstances that led them there."

Dennis cleared his throat. "To that end, we considered creating some kind of artificial environment for them. Replicate the look and feel of contemporaneous facilities. With just a tad bit of luck, their memories will all be intact. The last thing they'll remember is falling into the water. Let's say we wake them and pretend to be a neutral country that led a rescue mission. Someone who would be friendly enough with the Nazis to make them comfortable."

"Portugal," Emily interjected, "That's exactly what we were leaning towards, Emily. We invent a reason to keep them detained. It wouldn't be unusual for them to be subjected to a questioning after that. If it all goes well, we can get them to tell us their names, ranks, and the purpose of their mission. Emily can run whatever information we get through public records to confirm it."

George narrowed his eyes at Emily. She shrunk beneath his gaze. "Are you willing to do this?" he asked her.
She still seemed a little shocked from the day's huge revelation, but she gathered herself. "I am."
Butch smiled. "Then do we have a green light for the operation, Boss?", "See that it's done."

CHAPTER XIII

SOME ISLAND ASHORE OF EASTERN US COAST
April, the 18th 2015

"Kartoffen!" Daniel heaved. He looked at them all, so calm in their expressions even though they'd just told him the impossible. If they were telling the truth about, then the pieces all fit, but it seemed too much like something out of a science fiction novel. Real life couldn't have been like that. What about the war? Had they won? Then Daniel's thoughts turned to his family. If all these people said was true, then his family really had spent the rest of their lives wrongfully thinking he was dead. Daniel couldn't accept that.

The man who called himself George gave Daniel a puzzled expression. The woman next to him explained, "It's German for potatoes. Slang for bullshit. He doesn't believe us.", "How do you know that?" the other man, Butch, asked, "German calculus professor. Said it all the time when I made excuses for why I never completed my assignments. I've never been that great with math."

George raised a hand to silence the two of them. He looked sternly at Daniel. "Trust me, son, I didn't want to believe any of this either when I first heard about it. No IDs, no tags, no relevant marks on the submersible…you can probably imagine, that made me even more skeptical. But then Cristoph gave up his name and we had a start, even if it wasn't solid. But you, Daniel, you're the one who made this all come together. Once we learned your name, we made a major breakthrough."

"No, you're lying. How can any of this be true when I spoke to my son? If you're not lying, he would be…he would be older. But that was the voice of my little boy."

"Yes, it was the voice of your little boy. Franz Sommer. Seventy-two years old, worked honest jobs most his life, and retired in Bavaria. Still likes to stay active. It did take some deception to get him to work with us. We told him we were making a documentary about the missing soldiers of World War II. He was more than happy to tell us about you.", "Liar."
"Learning about *Alice and Wonderland* was another to add to the list of lucky strikes.", "You're lying!", "Why would we lie now," George challenged. We can't get any further with dishonesty."

"Whatever you're planning depends on me believing that, doesn't it?" Daniel wouldn't be swayed. Unless they could provide tangible proof that his boy was a senior citizen living out the rest of his life in retirement.

George puffed. "Can we please just show him for fuck's sake?", Butch replied: "Whoa, boss. When we agreed to do this in steps, we agreed on *little* steps. Is it really a good idea to show him that?"; George's answer was sharp: "Either we get him to believe us now, or we wait around for another seventy years.

Now, I don't know about the rest of you, but I don't have that kind of time."

Butch didn't argue any further. George seemed to have that kind of control over his subordinates, just like the Nazi high command had over German soldiers. Voicing concern was well and good as long as the concern didn't turn into disagreement.

"What are you about to show me?" Daniel asked, "You'll see when you see." Certainly, George didn't seem like the kind of guy to spoil a secret. He seemed frustrated enough that Daniel didn't believe him. But what did he expect? There were absolutely no grounds to believe he'd miraculously survived seventy years encased in ice. No scientific finding supported that kind of phenomenon. If they had, the Nazis would have known, It was a while before Butch reentered the room. George and Daniel both occupied the time with nervous tapping and twitching, and when Butch finally returned holding two thin panels affixed to a hinge, he opened his mouth in confusion. "What is that supposed to be?" he asked, trying to mask the fear that was beginning to bubble in his stomach.

"MacBook Pro," Butch answered. "It's a portable computer." He propped some of the fallen furniture and gestured for Daniel to have a seat. He complied. Butch put the device he called a portable computer—something Daniel knew couldn't be possible—between them. The backside of the MacBook Pro, as the device was introduced, bore a shiny outline of an apple with a single bite taken out of it. It was obviously a logo of some sort, but it seemed quite juvenile to Daniel that the military would represent themselves with an apple. There was no threat of intimidation. No one would fear an apple.

Butch fumbled around on the keypad which was miraculously attached to the screen of the device by the hinge, like a sideways door. Whatever it was he was doing, it ended with him heavily pressing a button on the keyboard.

"Hello, Sommer!" George said, but when Daniel looked up, the man's mouth was closed. He was grinning widely but definitely not saying a word. "The Reich is very proud of you!" There was no doubt about it. The voice was coming from the portable computer. "We are more than willing to welcome you back to Germany."

Butch pressed another key on the keyboard. Just as perfectly as George's voice had come out of the machine, General von Kleist's came through, loud and clear. It was a German translation of the phrase George had just spoken through the machine. Daniel turned it over in his head. They bugged the conversation, pulled a sound clip and had George repeat it in English. It was a simple trick. It could be done.

"Nein, you said you studied history. It would not be hard to find audio of the General.", George rolled his eyes. "You're quite the stubborn one.", "Takes after you, boss," Butch tossed in. He caught a deadly gaze from George and went back to fiddling with the computer.

"How about a demonstration?" George offered. He joined

Butch and Daniel at the table and clicked around on the screen using a finger pad. "It would not be hard to find audio of the General." He spoke those words clearly to the computer, enunciating every syllable properly, "It would not be hard to find audio of the General," the computer mimicked in Von Kleist's voice. George pressed another button. The sentence repeated again, this time in the voice of the Fuhrer. He pressed yet another button and the sentence repeated in the voice of his son.

George folded the laptop closed. "Since your rescue by the Portuguese, you have always been confined in rooms without windows. You've been blindfolded when transferred between those rooms. Everyone you have spoken to since that rescue has been an actor with the purpose of getting you two to reveal your identities to us under what you would consider normal circumstances."

Daniel heard the words but still wanted to fight them. He wanted to pretend that he'd never met these three people from the future or that he'd miraculously traveled to them from the past. Tears welled up. His family, his way of life, the war…all of it was done with, and he had nothing to show for it. He had no one to turn to and nowhere to go.

"My wife?" Daniel choked, "Remarried at the end of the war, bore two more children, and died in a car accident in 1967 along with those two kids and her second husband.", George said.

The story was too convenient. She remarried and had a

second life after Daniel, but conveniently died with it all. Those two children weren't alive to verify the story. After what Daniel heard, though, he found it increasingly difficult to remain a skeptic. The computer that could change voices made it perfectly clear how easy it was to deceive them. Cristoph had seen through it. He was a good solider. Now the two of them were reduced to less than that, "Who won the war?".

"Not the Germans," George laughed. "Hitler committed suicide with his wife on the eve of total defeat.", "What day is it?" Daniel gasped, They'd all been waiting for that question, all three of them worried for how Daniel would react.

Butch spoke the answer slowly, carefully. "Tuesday, April the eighteenth." He knew that wasn't enough. He paused briefly to compose himself. "The year is two thousand fifteen."

George jumped in. "I'm impressed Cristoph managed to piece together that we were deceiving the two of you. He's the kind of soldier who observes every protocol to a T. We imagined that he'd fall in line with a General. It never crossed our minds that he'd rebel so strongly."

"He had orders. The chain of command was supposed to give him exact dialogue. It was scripted. What your version of the general said wasn't part of that protocol."

"Beaten by German paranoia" - George shout - " But we shouldn't have been. Emily, you were in charge of the script, weren't you?", "Oh, don't look me like that," Emily scolded. "I put hundreds of hours of research into this. If I didn't know about the protocol, then no one did. The Germans kept the truth a secret and nearly died with it."

The Germans died protecting their secrets. Then the truth of the new reality dug deeper into Daniel's mind. "We lost the war."

"Yes. You did. And the world is a better place because of it. No more bickering between European countries. No more senseless territorial disputes. Everyone is quite friendly.", Daniel considered this for a moment. "If there are no records of our mission, then it was a success. That's how it's supposed to be."

"That is true," George sighed. "It seems that we undervalued the importance of your mission. It's also true that by now, it doesn't matter whether or not the details of your mission are made publicly available."

Emily shook her head. "I don't think there's anything to be made public. This isn't a comic book. No one will believe the story about these two men returning from the dead. Besides, I looked everywhere for info that would have been invaluable to our goal. No matter how many new, interesting secrets I uncovered, their submarine was never accounted for.", Daniel gasped: "That's good and fine. The only one who knows anything about the mission is over there." He pointed to Cristoph, still sprawled out on the ground without a clue what was going on."

"Daniel, war is over. You don't need to hide anything anymore. You're free from that responsibility." George placed his hand on Daniel's shoulder, as though that contact had the power to physically erase Daniel's sense of duty. It didn't, but it made the soldier feel more at home. George seemed more a guardian or father than an enemy or manipulator.

"All I know is the mission name," Daniel answered. And even that little bit of information was held too so tightly by German high command, I was grateful even to know that."

"That makes two of us, but knowing that the mission had something to do with German property doesn't really help us. It only makes sense that a German mission involves German property.", Daniel turned his head to the side. "What are you talking about?"

George looked over to Emily, then Emily looked to Butch. Emily spoke up. "The engraving on a leather folder we found in the safe aboard the ship was DDE. They're the same letters that were stamped onto the we found on the Captain's desk, right? It translates to 'German property,' right?"

"Who told you that?" Daniel asked suspiciously, Emily coughed. "We inferred it.", "You inferred wrong. The acronym is indeed the name of the mission, but it stands for Die Donker Engel.", "And how does that translate to English?" George asked, "The Dark Angel." was Daniel's prompt response.
The room filled with silence. It didn't match with anything they knew about either the time period or the mission. Admittedly, they didn't know much about it anyway, but it still came as a shock that they were so far off from the truth after all the effort they put into the plan.

George spun on his heels. "For the love of..." All eyes went to him. "Jesus, Emily. Bad scripts, incorrect translations.

Is *any* of the research right?" Then dead silence. "Okay..." George cleared his throat. "So now that we know what the abbreviation really means, what can you tell us about the mission? What were you doing out there? And what can you tell us about the boat's payload."

The men made Daniel feel important, like he had a larger role to play in everything. Sadly, no matter how intently they interrogated him, it didn't change how little his role played on history. "Nothing," he answered. "I was only serving as the navigator. Believe me, I tried to learn more about it myself, but it's like I said." He pointed to Cristoph again. "He's the only one who knows anything."

"But you were aboard the ship, were you not? You had to have seen or heard something!" George was getting fired up now. He refused to let all the hard work they did go to waste.

"I don't know how useful my story will be to you, but I'll tell you what I know."

CHAPTER XIV

KIEL, GERMAN NAVAL BASE
February, the 5th 1942

The beds in the Kiel garrison left much to be desired, but that was to be expected of the accommodations of any navy base. At the very least, the two men with whom Daniel shared the room had gone out earlier. By the time they returned home, he'd be blissfully asleep. Whenever officers went out drinking, things went on for much too long. For most men, it was easy during such tense times to get swallowed up by alcohol. Besides, it would be the last time they had to have fun until their deployment the next day. Daniel fully understood what drove them to go out. It wasn't alcohol he needed though.

Daniel looked out of his window at the stars densely cluttered in the sky. He could only hope that his wife and son were staring out at the same stars and thinking of him. Had he the chance, he would have spent his final night with his family, not holed up in some bar or flirting with local whores at the brothel. Those were temporary pleasures. Family was forever.

The Big Dipper was as distinguishable as ever, hanging off the body of the great bear. Daniel had spent many nights laying in the grass with his son, teaching him the names of stars and constellations and how to locate them in the sky. What he wouldn't give to do it one more time. At the present, all he could do was pull out the small picture from his packed bag. Simply holding it brought a smile to his face. In the picture, his wife and son smiled back at him. He tucked the photograph back into the bag, between two pages of *Alice in Wonderland*, the book he promised to bring his son when he returned from deployment.

Just as he was about to pull the book from the bag, the door to his room flew open. Three men marched in, looking entirely unpleasant. One was an officer, fully decked out in his uniform. As for the other two men, they dressed semi-formally. "Fuck," he mouthed. The ununiformed men were from the Abwher. If they were involved, something bad was happening. Between the three men, it was the officer who spoke first, "Daniel Sommer?" the officer asked, Daniel quickly checked the officer's decorations. "Yes, Herr Colonel." He stood at attention, "I'm going to need you to come with us. Right now.", Daniel took a tentative step forward. The colonel raised a hand to stop him: "You'll want to get your things together first."

Whatever was happening, Daniel didn't like the way it sounded. He turned to his bag, fully unzipped, and the book poking out of it. It was almost time for him to see his son, "You have five minutes, Sommer." The colonel looked at his watch. "Well," he shrugged, "you had five minutes from when that door opened. Now you're down to three and a half."

A colonel and two Abwher agents weren't people whose visitation he could treat lightly. No matter how much he hated them barging in and pulling away from his plans, he had no choice but to comply. Even so, it wouldn't be discourteous to ask for the purpose of their visit. "Where are we going? What do I need to bring?"

"Two minutes, fifteen seconds."

That made it clear enough that these men weren't to be questioned. Daniel zipped up his back, flung it over his shoulder, and looked around the room for anything else he might need. He hadn't brought much with him to begin with, but there was no telling how long he'd be gone. He double checked to make sure he still had the photo and book, and with that he was off.

The three men led him from the barracks to a car waiting outside. The two Abwher members got in the driver and passenger seats. Daniel sat in the back with the officer, trying to look forward and keeping himself from asking any questions that might get him in trouble. Whatever they wanted from him, it had to be quick business for them to pull him from the barracks so suddenly. That thought calmed him for a while, but when the car came to a stop at a closed-down dock, his concern resurfaced.

He recognized the dock. It had been closed down months ago and was officially declared off-limits to all traffic when the allies bombed the area only two weeks ago. Signs of the recent bombing remained although there seemed to have been an effort to rebuild some of the dock. Looking out onto the water, Daniel could see why: A submarine was chained to the dock. A small group of men rushed in and out, carrying things to and from it; The driver shut off the car engine, and the officer turned to Daniel. "Get out," he said plainly. "And move quickly."

Daniel didn't waste any time following the instructions. Once outside, he could taste the ocean air and smiled. He'd always felt at peace on or around water. But his peace was short-lived. There was too much wrong with the scene around him. Before anything else, Daniel noticed that the submarine bore no distinguishing signs. The metal looked clean, either brand new or recently refurbished. He thought he could even make out faint outlines where logos or insignias might have been inscribed. Then there were the men rushing in and out. Daniel hadn't thought much of them at first, but as they walked closer, he could see that they weren't actually loading anything onto the submarine. Everyone went in empty-handed and came out hauling something. Of those things, the most distressing were the torpedoes. It didn't make any sense. If they were about to go on a mission, why would they be removing their most important weapons? Daniel kept his concerns to himself. The Abwher were involved, so there must have been a good reason for it. The group came to the end of the road and stepped onto the wooden paneling of the dock; At that moment, a well-decorated man called over.

"Colonel Ziegler!" His voice boomed with importance, and Daniel knew immediately who it was. The group all turned around to see General von Kleist overseeing another group of officers. The colonel—Ziegler—broke off from Daniel and the Abwher to consult with the general. If Von Kleist was also there, things were far more serious than Daniel imagined.

The Abwher led him onto the submarine, onto the conning tower. From there, he could see Colonel Ziegler and General von Kleist clearly. But he didn't have much time to wonder about that because as soon as the Abwher made it clear that Daniel's duty was to the tower, they shoved him below into the room that was to be his prison. They wanted him to man the conning tower, but why? And why remove the on-board weapons?

There were rumblings in the submarine, the sounds of more things being shuffled around, and eventually it started to rumble. They were moving. Dread set heavily in his stomach. With so many hot shots overseeing the operation, his pleas would mean nothing. He was there. That meant they needed him. If he wanted to get back home to his family, he'd have to comply even if he didn't completely understand what they were doing. Unfortunately, that also meant that there was no telling how long the mission would last. He'd be god-knows-where doing god-knows-what for an indeterminate time, and that meant he couldn't know for sure when he'd be home. His stomach sank even lower.

Daniel laid down in bed, pulled out his copy of *Alice in*

Wonderland, and read to distract himself from the confusion unfolding around him. He spent a few hours like that when a heavy knock came at the door. It opened before he could invite his guest in. It was the colonel: "Good evening, Sommer.", "Good evening, colonel." Thus, ended the formalities; "Follow me," Colonel Ziegler commanded. Daniel complied.

They moved down the halls of the submarine. It was strange to see the submersible the way it was. Everything was so clean. The floors were spotless, the walls were devoid of any markings, and all the rooms seemed to be repurposed. On the trip to wherever the colonel was taking Daniel, they passed the radio room, oddly devoid of a radio. A bed had been moved into the room instead. What kind of a military operation required a submarine without weapons or a means of communicating with allies? If something went wrong...Daniel tried not to think about it. German high command must have considered all those things already and planned appropriately.

Colonel Ziegler led Daniel back out to the conning tower. There was another man already there, looking out at the ocean. "Good to meet you," the man said. "I've heard you're the best navigator in the navy, Mr. Sommer.", "I do my best, sir." Daniel looked up to the stars, the infinite little lights that could bring any sailor home safely if they knew how to read them. Many years before he'd ever enlisted, his grandfather had taught him the names of the stars and constellations. For a long time, that knowledge was a blessing. But now, it didn't very much seem so; "Sommer," Colonel Ziegler said, "in twenty-four hours, we need to reach this position." He pushed forward a piece of paper. Two coordinates were written out on the paper, but nothing else. They weren't relative to any other information; there wasn't a map, Daniel set to work immediately. He stepped in front of the other man, who he assumed must have been the captain, and took the instruments in hand. Looking to the stars, he began to set course. "I can give you an estimation. Do you have a pen?", the captain pulled one from his shirt pocket and handed it to Daniel who began to record notes on the paper. In a fit, Colonel Ziegler snatches the paper back from him. His eyes burst with fear and discontent, but he reeled himself in. He drew another pieces of paper from his pocket and handed that one to Daniel.

On this new piece of paper, Daniel finished writing out their course and handed it to the captain.

The man looked over it very briefly. "Impressive work. Three minutes to set course, and with exceptional accuracy. You have my compliments.", "Thank you, sir." Daniel then turned to the colonel. He hadn't expected the brusque man to offer a compliment of his own, but he would have liked to better understand the situation. Ziegler only stood there, face as set in seriousness as it had always been. He did, however, produce a lighter with which he set the paper with the coordinates alight. He drew a cigarette from a case and lit it with the paper before letting the paper drop to the ground and burn away.

Daniel took the chance to break the ice: "You don't

happen to have another cigarette, sir? I left my pack downstairs.", with a grunt, the colonel handed Daniel a cigarette and lighter, Daniel politely replied: "Thank you.".

Colonel Ziegler had barely smoked his own cigarette by then. More than half remained, but he tossed it into the sea. Then he looked straight at Daniel and said, "The less you smoke, the longer you live." He didn't stay around long enough for Daniel to respond, instead disappearing down into the belly of the submersible. Daniel turned to the captain: "Did I say something wrong?", the captain sighed. "I don't think so. I'm sure he's just nervous. This is the biggest assignment of his career. There's no telling what happens if he doesn't succeed."
It seemed like Daniel was the only one who didn't know anything about the mission. "The less we talk about it, the longer we live," he said, trying to imitate Ziegler's voice. He waited for laughter that never came. The captain's face turned deathly serious: "Exactly right. Now, the guards will escort you back down to your room. You'll be summoned when needed."

Daniel finished his cigarette before letting the men take him back down to the quarters they essentially had him imprisoned in. When he stepped inside, the door closed and clicked. They didn't have him here of his own will, and they knew it, so they locked him in his own room—a prisoner to his own country.

Daniel had nothing to do in his room besides sleep or read his book, but at the moment, he really wasn't in the mood, so he chose sleep. It wasn't long after finally dozing off though

that he was woken by a knock at the door: Ziegler stood in the door when Daniel got his eyes open. "Get ready," he said. "We need you now, Sommer.", by now, it was beyond him to question his place there. Daniel followed silently to the conning tower. The captain was still there, staring into the vast ocean. He only turned around slightly when he addressed him.
"Sommer, could you get our position please?"

Wiping the sleep from his eyes, Daniel took up the instruments to begin his calculations. The captain provided him a fresh piece of paper where he recorded the new coordinates. Again, he made the calculation in quick time; again, the captain gave his regards. But when he took the paper from Daniel, his face turned grim. Daniel stood anxiously, waiting for someone to say anything at all about where they were or why they needed to be here.

Expectedly, that's not what he got. The captain nodded a "yes" though Daniel wasn't sure what he was affirming. Ziegler seemed to understand perfectly though. He looked down at his watch and his face became grim too. Now the two of them stood there with Daniel on the conning tower, exchanging glances that Daniel had no hope of deciphering without any context. At that point, his patience ran out.

"Is something wrong?" he asked. Neither man answered. The captain went back to staring out into the ocean, and the colonel compulsively checked his watch, perhaps they were supposed to meet someone at those coordinates. It would explain why the captain stared out so intently: he awaited another vessel. And it also explained why Ziegler couldn't stop checking his watch: whoever they were supposed to meet with was late. This caused the both of them palpable concern; Daniel put his focus out on the ocean too, steady as it always was, carrying him along to territories unknown. The thought of the unknown made him nervous too. How long did they plan on keeping him captive on that boat, setting course while they withheld information from him?

Just then, something appeared, as though to assuage Daniel's confusion. It was a light. It flashed several times — a signal. There was a brief pause during which the captain and colonel drew closer to the edge of the railing, and shortly thereafter, the signal repeated. Daniel had been taught all the German signals and could recollect all but a few. This signal, however, was completely unfamiliar to him.

The captain turned, reaching for a high-intensity flashlight to signal back. He also pulled a small piece of paper from his pocket and began to unfold it. Daniel gleaned the letters DDE across its top before the captain realized he was still there. He started back, shoving the paper back into his pocket.

"Why the fuck are you still here?"

Ziegler spun around too now, eyes burning with anger and fear. "Return to your room immediately!" he spat. "This is a direct order from your commanding officer.", for the first time since arriving on the ship, Daniel felt just how small he was. Up until then, no one had actually ordered him to do anything. But now Colonel Ziegler stared him down, daring him to defy his command, and he understood just how huge a mess he'd been reeled into. Whatever was happening on that ship was bigger than he had any reason to be involved with. Daniel didn't waste any time doing what was ordered of him. He hurried to his room, closing himself in.

Several minutes later, he heard the lock click, again, they imprisoned him. He had nothing to do but return to bed, but now his mind raced with thoughts. He couldn't sleep. He could barely think straight, but all his thoughts were of the mysterious mission he found himself on. Everyone with knowledge refused to share it. How could they expect him to continue serving without knowing what his efforts were for? But of course they could expect it. He was a German soldier. He would die for his country before betraying it.

Daniel's thoughts were disturbed by an uncharacteristic movement in the submarine. A large group of soldiers were moving in ordered fashion down to the tail end of the ship. He heard their footsteps outside his door and heard their voices shouting occasional orders. Others spoke only with low voices, so Daniel pressed his ear against the door and listened close: very little made its way clearly to him, but the words *engel* and *donker* stood out. It was entirely possible those words were related to the lettering on the captain's slip. But Daniel had heard them in the wrong order. It made more sense as *donker* then *engel*, and more sense still if DDE stood for *Die Donker Engel*. It was possibly the name of the mission and the most information Daniel had regarding his current position. Keeping those words glued to the back of his head, he fell back into bed and slept through the rest of the night.

The next few days passed without incident. Every so often, Daniel was summoned to report on their position and quickly sent back to his quarters. Since signaling with the other boat, there was always an armed guard at the front of the submarine and an additional one right outside his quarters. The tides of the mission were turning. No one but Colonel Ziegler and the ship's captain seemed to be permitted in the front of the ship. Daniel only ever managed his way up there with both an escort and pre-approval. Their mission must have reached a critical phase.

Calculating their course was the closest Daniel could get to learning about their mission. From his coordinates, they were clearly on course for Greenland. The allies patrolled those waters. He couldn't imagine why German high command would risk sending a stripped down submarine that far into waters so heavily patrolled by the allies.

His answers began trickling in randomly one day when the Colonel called him to the conning tower midday with an informal message: "I wanted to let you have some fresh air and speak with you."; walking through the submarine now, Daniel was cautious and alert. He took deliberate steps and scanned around. That's when he realized just how much fuel had been loaded onto the submarine. Surely it far exceeded what they'd need for the mission. Where could they possibly be going that required so much fuel? Assuming the canisters were spread evenly throughout the submarine, Daniel figured it'd be enough to take them to Australia.

"What do you need to discuss with me, Colonel?" Daniel tried to keep his voice level despite his trembling legs, "I understand that I have been harsh…this may have made things difficult for you." The colonel seemed to struggle to move his lips to form those words, like conceding his hardness was a knife through his chest. Damaged or relinquished pride hurt more than bullets for some men. "In light of this, I'd like you to know you've done an excellent job so far. Moreover, you've mostly refrained from asking foolish questions." He looked sharply at Daniel. "I can see it in your eyes. You're naturally curious. You want to know more about this operation. Truth hurts, and the truth is that you cannot.", "Thank you, Colonel." "On to the heart of the matter. I am willing to propose your promotion once this mission is complete."; It felt like the weight of the world had lifted from his shoulders. To think that the colonel had called him out for *this*. "I'll do my best to earn your praise, Herr Colonel."

Ziegler seemed relieved that the moment ended. Daniel pulled a cigarette from his pocket and offered one to his commanding officer. Without words, Colonel Ziegler accepted the offering, and the two began to pull long drags from their cigarettes, each caught up in their own thoughts. The colonel made it halfway through his before reigniting conversation.

"Our mission has reached a critical point. We cannot afford to err from here on out.", "I understand." Daniel blew a puff of smoke out over the deck and watched it slowly diffuse.

The captain joined them shortly after, wearing a grim expression. Most likely, he was thinking the same thing as Ziegler, that their mission had reached a point where they couldn't afford to make mistakes. Daniel found it difficult to share those sentiments given how little he knew about the mission, once on the conning tower, the captain cleared his throat. Daniel nodded towards him, but the captain did not seem to notice. Either that or he didn't care. His attention fell solely on the colonel: "Everything is on track," he said; The colonel breathed in deeply and blew out. It was incredible to watch the way his whole body immediately freed itself from tension. Only after that did the captain give Daniel his attention. He pulled a slip of paper from his pocket and handed it to him.

"We need to reach these coordinates in twelve hours. I leave it to you to ensure we maintain the proper course.". The colonel looked at Daniel, perplexed. Seeing that look on his face, it registered with Daniel that there'd been something off in the captain's voice when he announced that order. Surprise, maybe? Something was happening behind the scenes that no one could tell him about, and the secrecy of it all was beginning to seriously unnerve him. If he was so important to the mission, he deserved to know something. But Daniel didn't let those thoughts escape him as words.

"Understood," he said instead. He took the coordinates and gave them a quick look over. That's when the surprise hit him too. The coordinates on the paper indicated that they were to travel south from their current position; in other words, in the opposite course they'd laid into all along. As far as Daniel knew, they hadn't discovered anything or made any advances that signaled any objectives of the mission had been completed. Moreover, the handwriting on the paper was completely different.

For once, all three men were confused. Daniel looked at both the colonel and captain and saw that neither quite understood what was going on. Their shared perturbation did little to ease Daniel's concerns. All this time, they'd been keeping him in the dark, but even they didn't know the full scope of the plan. It baffled Daniel that a man could captain a ship and not know his destination. And how was Cristoph to be expected to command when the objective of his orders wasn't clear even to him? He wanted to confront the two of them about the mission's secrecy, but he knew he couldn't voice those thoughts.

"Twelve hours then," the colonel said. "I expect this shouldn't be an issue for our navigator, should it, Captain?"; "I would not think so," the captain agreed, though both men couldn't shake the confusion from their faces.

Daniel didn't bother confronting them about anything or requesting a confirmation of the coordinates. He just went straight to work, flipping the paper over to the blank side and taking his position to observe the stars. In record time, he traced a course and relayed that information to the captain. The captain hurriedly took the paper from Daniel, scrutinizing the details of the route. With a nod of his head, he accepted it and disappeared back into the depths of the submarine.

Colonel Ziegler remained on the conning tower. "Your work is done, Sommer. You may leave. You'll be alerted of your new assignment in twelve hours."

Daniel complied. He found himself back in his room with nothing to do but think about the new coordinates. Nothing awaited them south except British waters in the heart of the enemy's naval forces. Allied powers would take care not to surrender those waters. They'd be littered with vessels equipped with state-of-the-art technology. And there Daniel was on a submarine stripped of all essential equipment, having just set them on course for certain death. He shook in his bed. Considering the captain's surprise at the coordinates, the instructions must have come from further up. As for the unfamiliar handwriting...it was evident that all of the coordinates had been provided ahead of time to the captain. He'd likely been instructed to read one at a time and only when the last was fulfilled. That would explain why he appeared to be frazzled by the instruction; But all that was conjecture on Daniel's part. He still knew as much about the operation as he did before: nothing.

The submarine had already resurfaced by the time Daniel woke the next morning. He assumed as much to be true from the moment he woke up, but it wasn't confirmed until two guards arrived at his door. Daniel sat up. He knew the routine.

Except this time, they blindfolded him before escorting him from the room. Daniel tripped several times along the way, and that only prompted the guards to force him more aggressively down the halls. However, the path was familiar. Daniel could have walked the path to the conning tower with his eyes closed. So far, that seemed to be exactly where they were taking him. Still, if that was the case, blindfolding him wouldn't be necessary.

Daniel's heart jumped. He pictured himself being tossed into the ocean, helplessly floundering towards the surface of the water then watching as the submarine sank back beneath the depths. Or maybe they'd give him a merciful execution. One shot to the head. Why else would they blindfold him? But no. That didn't make any sense. He was their only navigator. Without him, they were screwed. Besides, he still didn't know enough about the mission to warrant his death.

An answer came soon enough. Daniel kept on keeping track of his steps. As expected, they led him to the conning tower. Once there, the guards pulled the blindfold from him. First, there was bright light. Next, Daniel found the colonel and captain standing next to one another.

"Good day," the Colonel said. "We have the next coordinates prepared for you. We need to get there in eighteen hours." He handed over the slip on which the coordinates were written. Daniel gave it a quick look over.

"Straight north," he whispered, taking a glance at the surrounding waters. He almost expected to see an allied vessel or a plane soaring high above. He waited for the sound of weapons' fire that would precede their deaths. These were dangerous waters indeed. Not only that, the submarine was surfaced in broad daylight. He might not have felt so uneasy under the cover of night. Daniel looked over to the captain, who frowned: "We need directions quickly, Sommer"; It seemed they were always in a hurry as of late. Daniel did as instructed, plotting a hasty course. All the while, the colonel and captain glued their eyes on him, watching each step of his process. The sun had yet to snuff out the last stars, but a lot of Daniel's calculations were still guesswork based on the few stars still out and the their current coordinates.

The captain hurried to take a closer look at the charted course. He frowned, handing the paper to Colonel Ziegler. "If we go this course, we may not have enough fuel to return. Maybe if we tap into our reserves, it will be possible."

Something clicked with Daniel. If the captain had to think twice about using all the fuel on board the boat, that could only mean that the extra fuel wasn't ever intended to feed the sub's engines. They were carrying it for another, secret purpose.

Cristoph took a look at the course and nodded solemnly in agreement. "Absolutely not. We cannot use the fuel reserves for the sub." - "Then how are we supposed to make the return voyage.", Cristoph's answer came with a sinister undertone: "My dear captain, we may not have a need to return.".

The next words the captain spoke, he spoke through gritted teeth: "The way you speak, I'd think this was a suicide mission, Colonel."; Daniel's mouth began to fall agape. In all the time he'd spent on the ship, the captain had never undermined the colonel's authority, at least not so blatantly.

Quite contrary to the captain's reaction, the colonel offered the most level response Daniel had seen from him: "I am sure you have been briefed regarding your personal investment in this mission, Captain. I'm equally sure you have been instructed on how to proceed."; Now the captain's anger rose to the surface. "What personal investment?".

He had to ask, but Daniel felt like he already knew. It seemed that he was not the only member of the team over whom German high command held a dark cloud.

"My orders were to execute yours," the captain said. "That was all." - "Then that is what I expect you to do." The colonel's words were soft but sharp, and they cut at even Daniel.

"Forgive me, Colonel Ziegler, but I also took an oath in exchange for captainship that I would place the lives of my crew first and foremost. Surely, you wouldn't ask me to send the off on a mission with a one hundred percent probability for total loss of life." - "I appreciate your commitment, Captain, but this is not your crew. I am in command here. This is *my* crew. You would do well to remember that. You would also do well to remember that your livelihood when all this is over depends on your compliance. A negative report would not bode well for your career, nor would refusing me bode well for your family."

The captain flinched at the words, to hear that he was

nothing more than a figurehead on the ship. He refused to accept his position that easily though, even if it meant antagonizing Colonel Ziegler. He puffed out his chest. "I am captain here." - "In name, yes. We both adopted our ranks from the Fuhrer himself as soldiers in his army. However, since he personally assured me the full cooperation of the Kriegsmarine, I would expect you to be more forthcoming in your compliance."

Daniel couldn't believe what he'd just heard. From the look on the captain's face, neither could he. There was no way - Daniel simply could not imagine it - that Hitler personally gave Ziegler command of the mission. It had to be a bluff. The colonel could see that neither man in his company took him for his word, and he must have expected as much because his expression didn't change. He continued to exude that methodical calm as he pulled a notebook from his pocket, tore a page from it, and handed the page to the captain, who only received it reluctantly.

Morbid surprise washed over the captain's face. He handed the paper back to Colonel Ziegler and straightened up. Then he cleared his throat, turning over to Daniel: "I need you to cut some time from this course. Our top priority now should be reducing our fuel costs. Come with me. We need to discuss this."; Hearing this, the colonel smiled. "Excellent. See that it's done." He nodded to the guards next, both of whom had slipped Daniel's mind. They reapplied the blindfold and led him back into the depths of the submarine; But this time was different. Daniel had no idea where they were taking him.

He counted each step, recognizing that they passed the turn towards his quarters. They moved deep into the submarine from what Daniel could tell, deep into the backmost areas. Typically, the captain's quarters would be in the front of the submarine, but as had been clearly evidenced, this was no ordinary submarine. Moreover, the chain of command had been torn apart and reassembled; The guards eventually stopped prodding at Daniel. They pushed him forward a final time, and his arms brushed against the threshold of a doorway; Then he heard the captain's voice: "Leave us. I'll summon you when we're done here." The door slammed behind Daniel, then the captain removed his blindfold. They were in a rectangular room, complete with a rectangular table. The captain took a seat on the far side and motioned for Daniel to sit opposite him.

"Would you like some tea?" the captain asked. Daniel nodded cautiously. He wasn't sure why, but a creeping dread came over him. When the captain rose to prepare the tea, he took in more of the room. It was sparsely decorated. There was a large map just behind where the captain had been seated. He'd drawn lines across the map to indicate their course. It all looked familiar to Daniel and wasn't a bad idea at all considering the lack of onboard equipment. But something struck Daniel as odd on that map. The captain had drawn a question mark at the coordinates where the submarine turned south. It confirmed Daniel's suspicion that not even the captain knew the true objective of their mission.

And there was something else there: a thick folder with three letters stamped on the corner. DDE. Several other papers obscured most of the folder, so Daniel couldn't read any other text, but it seemed appropriate to assume everything he wanted to know about the mission was in that folder.

The captain returned with two cups of tea. "Thank you," Daniel nodded. Then he got quiet and leaned in to whisper: "Was that paper Colonel Ziegler showed you a direct note from the Fuhrer?" Daniel immediately bit his tongue, wondering what had emboldened him to ask such a question. If he wanted to see his family again, he needed to be compliant. Yet he also felt he'd never see them again if he continued to march towards what the captain called a suicide mission; "It wasn't anything like that," the captain answered, "but it seemed like it was." He shuffled some of the papers around on his desk, taking care to cover up the DDE folder. Daniel wasn't supposed to have seen it.

As for their ongoing conversation, Daniel puzzled at why the captain answered his question about the Fuhrer that way. Did he mean that the letter was a counterfeit? Daniel desperately wanted to know but he didn't want to risk his position on the ship by prying too deeply into well-kept secrets. There would be no immediate answer to that question as the door swung open.

A uniformed man trotted in, chin raised. The first thing Daniel noticed about the man was the insignia displayed prominently on his sleeve. Another colonel. That didn't make sense. There was no reason to have two colonels on the same mission. In fact, it was counterintuitive; Behind him, the captain gasped, quickly looking back and forth between Daniel and the newcomer. Daniel noticed this as well and cocked his head to the side; "Why the hell are you here?" the captain roared. "If Ziegler learns of this, we'll both be knee deep in shit."; This other colonel stumbled over his feet, a tinge of recognition of Daniel glinting in his eyes. He didn't need to be told again. The uniformed man disappeared through the doorway and pulled it shut; The captain sighed. "I apologize," he said. Daniel didn't dare question what just happened. Having two colonels would disrupt the chain-of-command.

From there, the two proceeded to their original plan of securing a more efficient route. It was tedious work, and all the while Daniel could see the captain stressing over the circumstances of their travel. Eventually, they did manage to work something out, and the captain called for the guards without another word about the mysterious note. Daniel was blindfolded and escorted back to his room where, yet again, he couldn't rest for all the questions racing in his head.

He had no more than eighteen hours until the ship completed its course. In the meantime he sat awake, staring at the ceiling, struggling to connect all the pieces of the mystery. In the first hours, he could feel the weight of the submarine shift as it changed direction. After that, it was mostly smooth sailing. They turned several more times, and Daniel knew their position by the order of turns from his revised route. At the last turn, he knew the journey was near its end as the last leg of the journey was relatively short.

Daniel's time was mostly spent between staring at his watch and the ceiling. He did manage to fall asleep for a few hours, but one of the submarine's turns had roused him from the light slumber. Now that they were on the last leg, there was no way he could sleep again. The submarine was very, very close to Greenland. By his estimations, they were just offshore, close enough to see the beach at least, were they to surface; It was an errant thought that Daniel hadn't seriously considered. To him, it had been a turn of phrase or point of reference, not a recommendation or prediction of events to come. Even so, he felt the submarine lurch unexpectedly. There shouldn't have been any other turns but they were definitely turning. Daniel couldn't mistake the feeling.

They went along the new course for a while much to Daniel's anxiety. According to his watch, they'd been in motion for well over eighteen hours. Wherever the submarine was headed hadn't been in his calculations. It soon got to that place and stopped. And then it surfaced, and Daniel's heart dropped; He shot up in bed. "Again?" But even that was just the tip of the iceberg. An ear-splitting sound rumbled the walls of the submarine. An explosion. Now Daniel knew that his fears were right. They shouldn't have come out there. He looked over to his bag and the book poking out of it. He needed to see his family again, his son especially. He didn't want to die there. He couldn't.

"Sommer!" Daniel whipped around. His door was already opening for Colonel Ziegler to step through: "Something has come up. We'll be needing your assistance." - "What's going on? I heard explosions?", "Never mind that." Ziegler motioned for Daniel to follow him. "You will take our position, and then you'll forget where we are. Understood?" Daniel didn't understand at all but nodded anyway. He reminded himself that if he wanted to survive, he needed to comply with the colonel's orders. "I understand." - "Good. Follow me."

Outside the confines of his room, people bustled about. Everyone was carrying fuel tanks and unmarked boxes which Daniel assumed must have also contained some kind of fuel. The colonel made him help transport the fuel and crates from storage up onto the conning tower. He did so without complaint and without question. At the end of the second hour, all the fuel had been reallocated. Thick beads of sweat dotted Daniel's brow; The work was long and difficult, and by the end of it all, Daniel's arms felt like jelly. One of the armed men escorted him back to his room where he was to stay until summoned again. He didn't mind the confinement this time. He could use the rest. But rest did not come easy. Every so often, he'd hear something outside, like a muted rustling. It wasn't until the third that he recognized them as explosions: "All that fuel…" he whispered to himself. No matter how much the captain and Colonel Ziegler tried to keep him in the dark, the pieces of the puzzle were beginning to come together in his head. They wouldn't have had any reason to move all that fuel unless they were close to shore or some other place where the fuel could be properly unloaded. Either a shore, he thought, or an iceberg. But why? If they were blowing holes in an iceberg, the fuel made sense. It would take an incredible amount of heat to bore a hole into it. The real question was what would be going into the hole. And why an iceberg. It was so discreet. How would they ever manage to find it again?

"Meteo station." The idea came to Daniel immediately, like a divine revelation. They'd been using him all this time to navigate, but if they were able to establish navigation stations discreetly throughout the ocean, they'd be able to move much more quickly. That had to be it. It would explain the secrecy.

Still, more questions raced through Daniel's mind. The goal of the mission didn't account for why the Fuhrer would be issuing direct orders to the crew—if those orders did in fact come from Hitler; and it certainly didn't account for the presence of the second colonel. Maybe the second colonel was there to oversee the station while Cristoph remained stationed on the U-boat. Things were certainly coming together. Daniel rolled over in bed, closed his eyes, and let the sounds of the explosions lull him to sleep.

Daniel woke to a knock at his door. When he opened his eyes, Cristoph stood at the end of his bed. The captain was behind him, standing in the doorway: "Wake up, Sommer. It's time to set course. The captain will take you to the conning tower."; Daniel absently wiped the sleep from his eyes and did as instructed, dragging his feet along behind the captain. Everything seemed to be business as usual. That is, until they arrived and Daniel saw one of the sailors already standing out on the tower, a pair of binoculars pressed loosely against his face. Even more peculiar was that the sun was still out, although there were still a few visible stars.

The captain cleared his throat. "There've been reports of icebergs in this area. Chart the course carefully." He extended a hand bearing a piece of paper. The new coordinates; For a moment, Daniel froze. They already knew that there were icebergs on a U-boat that had been stripped of all its equipment. It seemed farfetched that they could have happened upon that kind of data unless Daniel's supposition that they'd established a Meteo station was true. No matter what, he couldn't let on that he help those suspicions. Daniel accepted the new coordinates and went feverishly to work. Something was wrong though. Halfway through the task, he stopped: "Captain?" Daniel asked - "Yes?" - "Aren't we supposed to be going south? These coordinates take us north."

All of the color drained from the captain's face. He rushed towards Daniel, snatching the coordinates away. "Those must have been coordinates from earlier," he stuttered. "Ignore them." then he narrowed his eyes into such thin slits they might have been able to slice someone. "Ignore them."; Daniel's heart raced. "Yes, sir.", then the menace left the captain's eyes and he handed Daniel a new set of coordinates. "Use these." "Yes, sir." - "And Sommer?" - "Yes?" - "You won't mention those

other coordinates to anyone. Is that clear? This mission is almost at it's end. You would do well to keep a low profile."
Daniel swallowed, hard. "These are the only coordinates you've given me, sir. Due south." - "Good.", the Captain answered.

As Daniel worked on the course, the tension died down. The captain's breathing steadied and he eventually gave Daniel a playful pat on the back. "Stay out here. Get some air. You could use it instead of being cooped up all the time. I'll fetch you later."; Daniel nodded. When the captain left, he moved towards the railing and stared out into the sea. There were mysterious hidden on those waters. It was hard to know whether or not is was worth the risk to uncover them.

Just then, the man with the binoculars stepped back. "I'm going to head down for a bit," he said. "Do you mind staying up here? Look out for icebergs." - "Sure thing." Daniel waved the man away, then returned to the railing. He produced a cigarette, lit it, and let out a heavy sigh. His family was waiting for him. He couldn't risk cluing anyone in to how much he knew; "Damn the war.", he murmured, "Excuse me?" called a familiar voice, Cristoph's voice, from behind.

CHAPTER XV

SOME ISLAND ASHORE OF EASTERN US COAST
April, the 18th 2015

We collided with an iceberg along our course and then I woke up on a Portuguese ship - well, on your ship.".
The room was eerily silent: Everybody looked at each other, confused. It was an incredibly story. Telling it, Daniel hardly believed it had all happened himself, and he'd lived it. If nothing else clicked with the group, one thing did: the treasure everyone had sought after was false. George was the first to speak up on this matter:

"So what you're saying is that you went through all that trouble and you weren't hiding anything valuable?"; Daniel sighed, frustrated that this man still somehow thought he had the answers: "It's like I told you, nobody let me know exactly what the mission was. But I can assure you that if anything valuable was on that ship, it wasn't gold. It's more likely that it was carrying materials to build some kind of weather station or a shelter" - "And you're certain of this?" - "No, I'm not." Daniel motioned over to Cristoph who still lay unconscious. "He was the only one who knew everything."; Just as George was about to press the situation further, Emily cleared her throat.

"That actually makes sense. There are some incomplete documents that indicate the Germans wanted to plant meteorological sites in obscure territories. If those stations could transmit weather data to U-boats and other ships, the Germans would have an edge on the waters. And you said there was a lot of fuel on the boat, right Daniel?" – Daniel nodded: "Yes." and Emily continued: "A diesel engine would have been capable of recharging the Meteo stations. A submersible without navigation gear would be able to travel under the radar and recharge stations without being detected by Allied forces."

"That's just great," George muttered. "This whole thing has been a fucking disaster!"; Emily kept going: "Not necessarily. If there's any equipment left at those sites, it would be of great historical value."; George started to show being uncomfortable as the discussion was unfolding: "And what exactly can I buy with historical value? Is that a new currency?", Emily tried to mediate: "No sir, but—" - "But nothing! The only reason we concocted this plan was because you suggested they were carrying gold. Fuck! Do you know how much company money I embezzled to fund this goose chase? Do you? And my recompense is supposed to be 'great historical value?'" - "With all due respect, sir, I think you're misappraising the value of this discovery. I can tell you with certainty that…", George, clearly furious, took over the discussion: "Look here, little miss blue eye from the U-KAY; I don't care about your

Cambridge education or your PhD. I've got an MBA, and the B stands for business, not bullshit you lying bitch. Tell me, how does this bode for my business? Do you think I invested money in this just to see it go down the shitter? No, Miss PhD, I didn't. I invested it because I wanted *more* money, not historical value."

Daniel watched in shock as George fumed at the mouth, his chest heaving. Evidently, he invested a lot into the ruse. It was disappointing, sure, but not worth Emily standing wide-eyed, tears streaming down her face. Whatever it was that went wrong, he knew she didn't deserve that berating. George got aggressively close to her, fist clenched.

"Do you know what you've cost me, you stupid bitch?" Daniel thought he might even hit her, but the other man, Butch, who seemed to have some kind of influence over George, stood between the two before the situation escalated further: "Boss, it's not her fault. We didn't have all the information, and her guess at what was on that ship was the best we were going to get." - "Jesus, Butch, really? You should know how much I put into this. We spent money. *Money*. Tangible money. And for what? We're walking away from this empty handed.". Emily tried to convey the discussion on the most realistic hypothesis: "But the Meteo station….", George took over again: "What about it, huh? There's no gold! How valuable is a beat up station when our technology today can do ten times what theirs could? And the icing on the fucking cake is laying right there. We've got a corpse to clean up. Did you sign up for murder, Butch? Did you want to sling a body bag over your shoulders today, or did you want to sling a bag of gold over it?", then Butch tried to make his boss reasoning on the full picture: "Boss, calm down. Let's think through this. That guy officially died in the 1940s. No one is going to come looking for him. Also, there's something important in Daniel's story." Butch shot Daniel a grave expression. "You encountered another boat that wasn't one of yours, correct?" - "That's right," Daniel said; Butch turned pointedly to George and Emily: "I can't be the only one who thinks this is strange." When neither of them responded, he turned back to Daniel: "You mentioned that not even the captain was fully aware of what was going on. And that he fought against his orders." - "Correct. The route he gave was a suicide mission. He didn't want to follow it." - "And You also mentioned that you were…"

"Okay, stop there," George spat. "I don't have a PhD in history." He sneered at Emily when he said that and she, having endured enough of his abused, walked away to sit down next to Daniel: She didn't bother holding back the tears; Daniel provided her the napkin George had handed him earlier and helped her get herself together. All the while, George stood there self-assuredly, looking down his nose at her. Butch tried again to calm the tension down: "Come on, man, personal attacks aren't going to solve anything and neither will an ancient science experiment! There had to be something more important there. Why else all the secrecy. Why the unsanctioned rendezvouses? If two U-boats met, they had a purpose. And if they were only stopping in isolated, deserted areas, maybe they were experimenting with proto-nuclear weapons. I've seen something to that effect on documentaries."

Emily sniffled then gave an incredulous chuckle: "That would be even more significant historically!" George fumed out: "You say one more thing about history and you won't have a job. Is that clear?"; Emily shrunk back in her seat. It most certainly was clear. But then she caught a second wind of boldness and rose to her feet: "You can't fire someone for such a ridiculous reason in the UK. And watching the history channels doesn't make you an expert, just so you know. Doesn't earn you a Ph.D., that's for sure." - "Welcome to America baby, where history is on TV and I can fire you for whatever reason I choose."

"If I may," Daniel cut it. "Butch might be on the right track. One of the coordinates we received was in unfamiliar handwriting. Up until then, I'd been assuming that all the coordinates were written out by Cristoph as we moved in real time and immediately disposed of after I set the course." - "That's what I was trying to get at," Butch confirmed. He turned triumphantly to George, who didn't share in his enthusiasm.

"So now you're trying to tell me that someone from the other boat wrote out the next coordinates." - "Yes, that's a possibility." Butch trailed off. "But it still doesn't explain why they went north." - "Obviously this Daniel guy wasn't as good at his job as everyone gave him credit for."; Daniel read the spite in George's eyes. He could sympathize with the man for putting so many of his resources into a failed experiment. After all, Daniel had done the very same thing on the German U-boat. He sacrificed everything and got nothing in return. Even so, it seemed they were getting closer to solving the mystery: "Believe me, I mapped the courses as perfectly as could be done with the equipment I had."

Butch nodded. "Then there has to be something there. They wouldn't have gone through all of that for nothing. Especially if they needed two colonels for it." He turned to George: "Listen, Boss, I know we've already spent more money than we were willing to on this thing, but we're so far into it already, why not go ahead and see it through to the end? What difference will one more percent on the final bill make when there's still a chance we can recoup some of it?"

George sighed and found a seat. He held his hands over his face to encase his nose and mouth, and he thought for a long while. Everyone watched him expectantly. The only sound in the room was Emily's still-heavy breathing until George finally came to a decision. He turned to Daniel. "Would you be able to take us there?" He asked. - "What do You mean?", Daniel replied with a puzzled expression on his face; "To the place where the shelter, or whatever was, you built seventy years ago is. I'm asking if you could bring us there." - "As far as my memory serves, it's only been two weeks, sir. They're the same coordinates the captain showed me by mistake. And yes, I still remember them."

Emily chuckled, shaking her head at the strangeness of it all. Only two weeks ago, the man sitting next to her had been in the midst of a historic world. Two weeks ago, she'd been in a modern office, scrutinizing the details of documents from the time he'd been in two weeks ago. She found herself smiling softly in Daniel's direction; Daniel found himself smiling back.

It was George's voice that pulled them out of the strangeness and plunged them back into reality. "Everyone get your things. This will be the last leg of your mission, Daniel."

CHAPTER XVI

SOMEWHERE IN NORTHERN ATLANTIC OCEAN
April, the 23th 2015

Daniel thought for a moment that the cigarettes he pulled from his pocket were no longer in production. They hadn't been for a very long time. The ice had kept them relatively fresh though. He lit one and took a heavy drag. The smoke didn't move as smoothly down his throat as he expected from the brand, but he couldn't dispute the rush of nicotine that cleared his head as he stared over the edge of George's company ship. It cruised over steady waters towards Greenland where, if everything panned out, their prize waited.

But what weighed heavier on Daniel's mind than treasure was all the differences between the last time he sailed those waters. George's boat itself was an incredible machine. They'd passed several others along the way and Daniel's first reaction had been to hide away. He was still new to the idea of traveling in friendly waters. There was much, in fact, that he was new to. They'd spent several days preparing for the trip to Greenland; in that time, Emily had requested that a team of psychologists and historians assist in his rehabilitation and reeducation. The modern world was a much different place than the one he remembered; As Daniel went over the circumstances of his new life, Emily climbed the stairs out to the deck. She stood next to him: "Hey, how's it going?", Daniel turned and smiled. "So far, so good." - "Good. You wouldn't happen to have another cigarette, would you?", Daniel raised an eyebrow, Emily, a bit surprised, reacted: "You don't have to.". - "No, it's not that. I just didn't know you smoked. Here." He fished a fresh cigarette out from the package and placed it between her lips. He pulled his lighter from the other pocket, and lit the end. Emily inhaled sharply and blew out: "Thank you." - "No problem. I could use some company before my next treatment."

That's what they were calling his rehabilitation: treatment. It made him feel like he was sick, like there was something wrong with him. But while Daniel stood there looking disgusted with himself, Emily beamed in his direction. To her, he was the most valuable discovery of them all. Every day, he watched a curated program that detailed the significant events of each year since the disappearance of the German stealth sub; and every day, he was in awe at just how much he'd missed.

"How far along are you?" Emily asked, "1963." Daniel blew out a wisp of smoke; "You must be overwhelmed by the telly." - "Excuse me? The telly?" - "No, excuse me. You've probably heard the American term more often: The TV. In Britain, we call it the telly." - "Yeah, it's definitely overwhelming for sure. In my day, we had the cinema, but to think people now have that kind of technology in their homes—and in such a compact form. It's unheard of."

Emily continued: "For me, I can't imagine a world without mobile phones and Internet. And you, you've skipped right over all the little innovations that brought us here. You landed right at the peak of it.", then, she bitten her tongue, realizing that she unveiled two concepts that would definitely be unheard from Daniel, who caught the terms anyway and started asking: "You mean you can bring a phone along with you nowadays? Wow! and what's the Inter…net?"

Emily paused to take a few lofty drags from her cigarette. "Sorry I shouldn't spoil anything to you, but those things are so familiar and natural to me that they literally slipped off my tongue, where are you in 1963?" - "The very beginning. I just finished listening to Wallace's speech as the Alabama governor.", Emily looked puzzled but terribly interested: "You'll have to forgive me, I'm not really an expert on state politics in the Americas. Could you explain the speech to me?" - "It's a little muddy in my head, but I can give you the general points: Essentially, Wallace claimed that segregation between blacks and whites would last forever. It was disturbingly similar to my Germany. Mistreatment of people, riots in the streets…it reminded me of concentration camps. I'd been to a few of them, and they were some of the worst places I've ever been. I've never been a Nazi, Emily."

Daniel sighed, tossing the butt of his cigarette into the ocean before lighting another. "I never wanted to be one either. I saw the propaganda and heard the speeches from the leaders.

It's something I never wanted to be a part of. Those speeches I heard in the 30s and 40s were no different than some of the speeches from American leaders in the 60s.". Emily nodded at this, fully engaged by Daniel's passion for the topic; Daniel continued: "They persecuted the blacks no differently than Germany persecuted the Jews. It's depressing that twenty years later, there were still people who clung to that ideology. If I knew back then that it was wrong, how could everyone else still be in the dark years later?"; Emily, impressed by Daniel's sensitiveness, replied: "Historically, people cling to old ways of thinking. It's comfortable. It's safer than having their ideas challenged because it would mean that their entire lifestyle was fundamentally wrong. No one wants to think that about themselves."

Daniel nodded. "That does make sense." His eyes narrowed at the distant ocean, as though he were looking for something. "Even so, if we don't challenge ourselves, we'll never get better. I have a question, Emily." - "Yes?" - "Are things still that way? Are there still cultures like my Germany or 60s America today? I know I'm not supposed to be looking too far ahead of schedule, but I have to know. Germany was beaten in the war, but if things haven't changed, I have to wonder if it even matters *who* won."

"Of course it matters," Emily said sharply. She clearly didn't want to divulge too many details. Daniel could see the restraint by the way her mouth twitched and the way her eyes searched for the right words. "Racism still exists," she finally said. "In many countries, groups of people are still being subjugated. But we've still made a lot of progress. It shouldn't hurt your rehabilitation to know this much: the current president of the United States is a black man. He's the first black president in history, and he proves that people are becoming more accepting."

Daniel looked relieved: "Hm. So it seems like people are getting better, even if the process is slow. I can only hope the current president is as good as Kennedy.", Emily tensed up and Daniel perceived it: "What's wrong?" Daniel asked her. She only shook her head and said that it was nothing to worry about. She was hiding something from him, he knew, but he decided not to press the issue; She then broke the embarrassing silent moment: "I can't wait for you to catch up on your history. There's so much I want to ask you, so many holes in history you could fill." - "Trust me, there's a lot more questions I have for you." Daniel frowned. "Most of them, you can't answer yet, but I look forward to when you can." Now he smiled at her, and she smiled back, snuffing the butt of her cigarette on the railing before tossing it into the ocean.

Emily thought now about the Moon Landing, this will definitely be a surprise for someone who just knows the history of mankind till 1963: "There is one thing I'd like to tell you, but you can't tell anyone that you know."; Daniel blew a puff of smoke. "What is it?" - "It's something you'll see in six weeks, in 1969….", but the conversation ended there. George stepped up onto the deck and cleared his throat.

"Emily!" he barked. "Aren't you supposed to be preparing a report for me right now." He crossed his arms sternly. Emily, clearly embarrassed, replied: "Yes, I was just having a chat with Daniel…" - "This is not a pleasure cruise. Stay focused.", Emily sighed and made her way back below deck, but as she passed him, he stood in front of her: "I expect it to be ready tomorrow morning. And none of that technical babble. Write it so that I can understand it. OK? I need to know what can be monetized." - "Of course. You'll have it tomorrow morning." She tried to continue down the stairs but George stopped her again: "Oh, and by the way," George said before moving in close to Emily, "stop flirting with him. He's old enough to be your grandfather." Then he did something strange. He smiled, awkwardly, at her, for the first time since She met him, he was looking not as threating as he usually did; Emily laughed, no less awkwardly than George had smiled, thinking for a second that he was trying to flirt with her, "Old people aren't so bad, George. Their wisdom is charming." - "If you say so." - George straightened out his jacket - "I'll see you tomorrow, Emily. You're free to go."

CHAPTER XVII

SOMEWHERE IN GREENLAND
April, the 27th 2015

There was more ice in Greenland than Daniel had expected. Sheets of it stretched for as long as the eye could see. He stood on the shore along with George, Butch, and Emily. Dozens of George's employees were hard at work, spread across the expanse with presumably expensive equipment. Some scanned the ground with fancy-looking metal detectors. Others watched the sky as incredibly small flying machines hoovered well overhead. Daniel could hardly fathom how technology had evolved so much.

"What exactly are those flying machine-bird things?" he asked Butch - "Uhh…well, they're called drones. You control them remotely to survey an area.", Daniel looked very astonished and replied: "How is something like that even possible? When were they invented?", "A while," Butch answered, trailing off. He bit his tongue; "Hey!" George called them to attention. "Does this look like the time for chatter? Daniel! Stay alert. Does any of this look familiar?"

"I don't know." Daniel squinted and scanned the area. "It looks different than I remember. But I'm sure the bunker must be somewhere nearby"; One of the field technicians moved briskly toward the group, holding one of those apple-branded computers between his arms. Just as he began to speak, Daniel cut him off.

"Actually, I have a question. What's that apple on your computers mean?" - "Computer brand," George said dismissively.

Computers had been part of the reeducation program, but Daniel had yet to see one so small and sleek. The ones he remembered were mammoths of machines, filling entire rooms. Now they could be easily carried...and there were miniature helicopters that could be steered from the outside. Times had indeed changed rapidly.

The technician cleared his throat. "George?" - "Yes, go on." - "Drone 32 is picking something up." - "Where?" - "Fifteen hundred meters slightly northeast." - "Lead the way." George pushed the technician forward.

Everyone hurried in the direction the technician led them. A group of staffers had already gathered there, most of them probing the ground with their metal detectors. A long series of beeps confirmed the technician's information; George's eyes lit up. "Start digging."

Daniel stepped back from the digging men. He pulled a cigarette from his pocket and lit it up. Just then, George tapped his shoulder and nodded towards the cigarette pocket. "Didn't know you were a smoker." - "Doesn't hurt when I'm nervous." - "It seems like you've been nervous this whole time." Daniel waited for a laugh or a chuckle. Even a slight smile. But it never came; "I was concerned," George answered. "But now that we're so close, it's hard not to be nervous about what we'll find."

Emily approached as well, also in search of a cigarette. She got one from Daniel and promptly lit it. "Have you read my report?" she asked George; "Haven't had time. Give me an overview"; Emily let out a frustrated sigh. "Either they were hiding loot, doing scientific research, or setting up a meteo station.", George replied without looking at her: "As long as we can monetize it, I don't think I mind which of those it is."

By now, the dig team dug up enough ice to unearth an edge of the bunker. There was a large commotion and increased productivity after that. The bunker quickly took shape in the ice; George approached, standing on the edge of the ice: "Can we use explosives to speed this up?" - "We'd risk damaging whatever's in there," Butch protested; George took a large drag of his cigarette then tossed it behind him. "Let's hurry this up then.", Butch replied: "It would be best to find a door." Then he turned to the technician: "Is there any way to infer the layout?" - "We've got probes in the area. All we can really tell is how damn huge this thing is at this point, but we should be getting more specific details soon." - "Good." Butch gave the technician a pat on the back, then pulled Daniel several feet away from the group.

"How do you feel?", Butch Asked; "Strange. It feels like it's just been a few weeks. But it's really been seventy years since I've been here. It's a very strange feeling."; Static buzzed on a nearby technician's radio. "This is drone pilot seventeen," a frantic voice said. "We've found the door. Prepping minor explosions."

Several meters away, Daniel watched George rush towards one of the technicians, snatched the radio from his waist. "This is George. You are clear to go.", there was hardly time between George giving the order and the sound of the explosion blowing a hole in the bunker door.

CHAPTER XVIII

SOMEWHERE IN GREENLAND
April, the 27th 2015

George walked in first, head craning for clues. Next was Daniel and Butch. Emily went in last, notepad in hand. The bunker's internals were well-preserved considering it'd been there for seventy years. The few bodies the group encountered were frozen solid.

Surprisingly, Butch was even more excited at the insides than George: "This place looks like a time capsule. I remember making one when I was in college. I've completely forgotten where it is now though.", he said; "What's a time capsule?" - Daniel asked - "It's a box filled with iconic modern items. You bury it and future generations dig it up to see what people in the past valued."

They continue investigating the bunker, having found nothing noteworthy in the first few minutes of their exploration. As they pass another body, George bends over to observe it. "They've been well frozen. This guy still looks alive. Just look at his face." The corpse belonged to a uniformed man with a wide-eyed expression. George pulled the flashlight from his pocket and shone it into the man's eyes.

"You don't think..." Butch started - "We were lucky once. Maybe we'll get lucky again.", Butch looked for a moment at Emily who was rolling her eyes, together, they chuckled at the scene of George checking whether the frozen man he was lighting up the eyes of was hibernated as Daniel was, Daniel looked at them amusedly.

George turned the flashlight off and continued on his way. Daniel passed the corpse slowly, taking a long glance at it. He recognized the face as belonging to the second colonel from the U-boat. He stared at the colonel's face for a long while. Two weeks, he thought. But realistically, this man had been frozen for seventy years.

"Daniel!" Butch called from the distance; "I've found something!", Daniel ventured down the halls of the bunker until he found Butch and George, the former holding a thick, leather-bound book in his hand. Upon closer inspection, he spotted a Swastika on the front cover. Butch flipped through the pages, revealing a series of diary entries, all written in German. Most of it was burned beyond recognition, but when Butch landed on the last page, they all leaned in. It was perfectly readable. Daniel snatched the diary away and began translating; But before he gave his audience the English version of the diary's contents, Daniel made sure to give the whole page a quick look over, and several details immediately caught his attention. There was mention of another colonel and gas reserves, two details that were all too familiar. It was a big possibility that this diary belonged to the other colonel, the man who lie frozen just down the hall from where they stood now.

"Go on!" George urged, leaning in close and squinting at the words even though he could not read them, "Okay, okay. Here goes." - Daniel cleared his throat - "This is a rough translation", and Daniel started reading…

CHAPTER XIX

SOMEWHERE IN GREENLAND
April, the 30th 1942

It is clear to me now that the German army has no intention of coming to rescue us. Our gas reserves, despite numerous calculations that determined they would last for two months, have been depleted in sixteen days. It took us too long to realize the gas would not last us. I did everything I could to stretch what remained for these final days and have even set fire to a number of documents, including much of my written account of this mission, to keep us warm in these last moments. I fear this page may be the only record of what terrible fate has befallen these men. It is my hope that it will be found and the honorable sacrifice made by the men here will be known to all.

In the event that we could not survive down here, I was ordered to kill everyone on board as a state-suicide. I am a soldier, but I do not murder in cold blood. Whether I kill us or not, we will die. We signed up for something far bigger than us, and this is our reward.

As a soldier in the Wehrmacht, I've witnessed the horrible war crimes committed on the eastern front. I've seen the elderly slaughtered and young children shipped off to camps to be tortured and murdered en masse. It is my fortune that I've never been asked to commit such atrocities, and I will not tarnish that record now by actively murdering my comrades. Even so...I cannot shake the feeling that I'm no better than those who murder indiscriminately, as I have completely failed in my duty to see these men home safely.

I can only hope that our sacrifice will make a dent in history. If not...then may God have mercy on us all"

CHAPTER XX

SOMEWHERE IN GREENLAND

April, the 27th 2015

Everyone stood still and silent in the room. Their breaths were shallow, reserved. And Daniel, still holding the diary up to his face, turned over its contents again and again, trying to fit it within the larger context; Butch was the first to speak: "Poor guy," he mumbled, shaking his head; "Him?" George scoffed. "The poor guys are the corpses all around us. Hell, we're the poor guys. All this and we haven't learned anything new about the mission. All we have are these bodies, and some cutlery over there…miscellaneous objects scattered around." He turned in a circle, pointing out every useless piece of information he could find. Everyone else stared on dejectedly as he did so. Then, he stopped circling and pointed out two bodies: "But I must admit, it's odd that these guys are wearing different uniforms."

"British," Daniel replied immediately, George gave him a very puzzled expression: "Wait, you were fighting the British in the war. Why would their officers be here?"; Daniel's expression turned sour. "Look there, under that one's arm".

"Ah." Butch approached and crouched next to the bodies. He lifted the arm in question, revealing a worn manila folder. He pulled it open and mouthed silently as his eyes scanned the contents. The longer he looked on, the wider his eyes grew; "Out with it," George demanded, stepping around to view the documents over Butch's shoulder. "What is it?" – Butch replied: "It's a map. Of the northern Atlantic it looks like. Not only that..." He looked up to Daniel. "There's a course set!"; Daniel didn't need to be instructed on what to do. He took the map from Butch and checked over the coordinates. "Yes!" he exclaimed. "This is perfect!"; "Perfect?" George stammered. "Give me more than that." - "These are the coordinates we set. If you look here, this is exactly where we met up with the other boat. These coordinates lead from that rendezvous point.", Daniel said.

"You're telling me the Germans met with a British ship?" "Makes sense," Butch added thoughtfully - "That would explain why they weren't using German signals. They didn't know them." - "That's right!" Daniel said excitedly. "And this handwriting is familiar. We're getting closer to the truth of things".

That may not have been a big deal for George and the others who were in it for profit, but Daniel needed closure. He had to know what the secret mission was that cost him so much, Butch was the first one to break the odd silence: "Alright, everyone together. Let's recap. Daniel. You were stationed on a U-boat that departed from Kiel to meet up with a British ship—most likely a ship commissioned for its mission with the utmost secrecy—and this rendezvous was scheduled to occur at the coordinates written on this map." - "That's correct", Daniel nodded, "and the British were giving us the next set or coordinates for our voyage." Daniel trailed off, his voice slowing as his eyes widened; Then, he snapped and spun to face Butch. "That makes perfect sense! That's why we bore south then back north. The British seamen we communicated with provided us with a safe route through the Allied forces' patrols in the Atlantic." - "Why not just give your ship clearance to pass through?" George asked, "Impossible!" Butch answered - "Tensions were too high between the Allies and the Axis. There's no way they'd be allowed safe passage. Besides, this mission was probably as much of a secret on the British side as it was on the German side. Few people knew anything at all about it. Even fewer people, if any, knew the full story.", George shook his head: "This is ridiculous. It goes against everything we know from history.", Emily nodded her agreement: "…To think Germans and Brits were working together in the midst of the war…", "Yeah," Butch murmured. "But we've got the bodies here as proof. Whatever they were doing, they were doing it together."

Now Daniel put in a few words of his own. "I think this other German colonel arrived on my boat from the British vessel." - "Fine!" George threw his hands up - "Let's just assume all that is true. It still doesn't explain what they were doing here in the first place".

"Well..." Butch started, "there's more in this folder." He shuffled through the papers until a series of laminated documents caught his eye: "Geez, looks like a Matryoshka..." He handled the papers with great urgency, running over each of them quickly before flipping to the next. With each paper, more color drains from his face; "What is it?" George demanded; Butch refused to answer. He only stared wide-eyed, deep in thought, at the space in front of him and handed the papers off to the others.

Everyone gathered around the papers now. Daniel took them cleared his throat and took center stage to read the contents of the them.

CHAPTER XXI

LISBON, GERMAN EMBASSY
February, the 3rd 1942

Herein is written in accordance with prior negotiation the agreement between the British Empire and the German Reich to meet the conditions of a long-term armistice. The German Reich, based on the prior negotiations mentioned above, already surrendered the deputy Fuhrer Rudolph Hess to the British Authorities as escrow; likewise, the British Empire will deliver a member of their royal family into the custody of the Reich. The member in question shall be Prince George, Duke of Kent. The member in question shall be transferred from British to German care during a naval exchange.

Strict guidelines are to be followed in the fitting of the vessel upon which the member in question shall be delivered. Firstly, the vessel must be stripped of all radio technologies and any other traceable communication devices. Secondly, the ship's crew must remain unaware of the true objective of the rendezvous.

Once the exchange is complete, German forces will transport the member in question to an undisclosed location decided upon by a small joint committee including no more than two ranking officers from each sovereignty. This location shall be kept secret until the armistice agreement is made public; upon publication of these terms, the British Empire shall receive clearance to collect their member in question. They shall also assume responsibility for salvaging the German crewmen who will be accompanying the member in question at that location.

The agreement will go public on April 30th, 1942. The German Reich will officially cease all aggressions towards the British Empire beginning on May 1st, 1942. In exchange for cooperation, the Reich shall see to resetting the Empire's borders to their designations prior to August 31st, 1939. On May 2nd, the Empire shall formally join the German state in its campaign against the Soviet Union.

The contents and conditions of this agreement shall be kept in the custody of a member of the British royal family for the entirety of the operation's duration to prevent its contents from leaking to public ears before all arrangements have been set forth.

CHAPTER XXII

SOMEWHERE IN GREENLAND
April, the 27th 2015

There was silence for a moment; "That's it," Daniel announced. "That's all it says."; "No way!" George said, stroking his chin as he did. "You're telling me that we're in the same room as Prince George, member of the British Royal Family?", "His corpse at least" - Butch chuckled - "Those papers are signed by both Hitler and Churchill. It's legit."

George looked really puzzled by what he just heard: "So a member of the royal family just disappears and no one asks questions. It never gets mentioned by historians. How the hell did they get away with it?" He turned to Daniel, eyes narrowed, who replied candidly: "How should I know? By the time he disappeared, I was already frozen."

"They wouldn't have to cover it up," Emily added. "The official story is that Prince George died in 1942 in an air crash; as for Rudolph Hess, his flight went immediately public, probably because Churchill, not fully trusting the Germans, wanted to push them to a point of no return".

"Whoa…" George said thoughtfully, then turned to Butch:

"We need to go public. If we bring this news to light, stocks will skyrocket. Business will boom. If we play our cards right, we can get the U-boat converted to a museum. Emily, gather all the information you can about this. Get preparations underway. Oh, and you can leave your job at the University, trust me, I pay way better", he concluded smiling.

Emily's answer left everybody in the room quite surprised: "Actually, George, I don't think that's going to happen."; The thoughtful, investigative Emily that Daniel had come to know wasn't the one who said that. She looked entirely different under the weight of the revelation, George looked at her being quite confounded: "What's that supposed to mean?"

Emily, with a kind of poker face, answered: "It means we've been looking for that U-boat and this place for over seventy years"; "We?" Butch asked. "Who is *we*?"

Emily didn't need to answer immediately. There was a humming sound that appeared in the background, faint at first. But over the next few seconds, it became very distinct. It was the hum of helicopters. Emily smiled twistedly. "Me and the guys outside." With that, she made her way to the exit. The rest of the group exchanged puzzled glances, then decided silently to follow her outside. None of them were prepared to emerge back into the open world just to find themselves surrounded by dozens of men, most of whom held weapons pointed at the group.

"What the hell is going on?" George demanded; Emily stood behind a group of her goons, well protected. Her head was only visible in the space created where two soldiers' shoulders touched, "Can't you tell."; "Double cross!" Butch spoke through gritted teeth; Emily blinked at Butch and continued: "You always were the smart one. We've been following you ever since you sent that first email regarding the U-boat. And when you needed an expert in history, my employer sent me to dig up more info."; "And who exactly the hell is your employer?" George asked - "I would have thought it'd be obvious by now. I work for MI6. Like I said, we've been looking for that document you're holding."

George was feeling deeply uncomfortable, but he tried to not let it transpire: "Oh? I suppose you'd like to take it from me, then." - "Yes, I would." Emily sharply replied.

Soldiers began rushing into the bunker and exiting with bodies and documents - whatever they could get their hands on, Emily concluded: "In fact I'm taking everything" - "So you're going to kill us?" George asked, Emily smiled and said: "And leave behind a trail to lead others to this discovery? Not likely." - "Okay," George intoned. "Then explain to me how you can be sure we won't go public with this anyway?"

Emily didn't have time to answer. Soldiers marched out of the bunker with the last of the documents and the last of the soldiers stopped short of the entrance to get George's attention. "If you don't mind," he said with a thick British accent, extending his hand; George considered refusal very strongly, but a nudge from Butch brought him to his senses. He relinquished the documents.

Seeing the way George's entire composure shifted, Emily let out an arrogant laugh. "For the record the last one who threatened us to go public with this was Herman Goering, and anyway what evidence do you really have, little George?" - "The U-boat!" he fumed. "All the people involved in this. We have a living witness for Christ's sake!" - "As for the U-boat, it bears no distinctive or otherwise incriminating markings. You let me inspect it very carefully, after all. And witnesses?", Emily scoffed, "Without any real evidence, you people can claim whatever you want. Scream it to the skies. Alert the press. Do whatever you will. Without any evidence, no one will take you seriously. So, go ahead. Do it if you'd like to tarnish your reputation, they will take you as seriously as people shouting conspiracy theories on the internet, and by the way, you might be surprised by how many of them are actually very close to the reality".

At some point during Emily's short speech, George's fists clenched. Veins were beginning to pop up on his neck. He looked like he was ready to lash out at the soldiers. But he still had one last card that she hadn't addressed; "What about him?" He pointed toward Daniel.

"You'll never see him again, that's for sure. He's coming with us." - "Going with you where?" - "Don't use that tone with me, George. You're not in control here, and I don't owe you any answers. Anyway, surely you must know that information is classified." - "Classified my ass! That's a human be…"; George choked on those words. The ice beneath them all shook violently and behind them, they could all hear the sound of explosives being detonated. The bunker was gone.

Emily smiled coyly. "Your mission is complete, Daniel. Please come with us now."; Daniel didn't have a choice, and he knew it. He turned to face the men and women who had accompanied him on the journey to answers. They'd finally found them, even if there was nothing they could do about it. "Well, guys. I have the answers I was looking for. This time period is new and strange and I don't think it's my place to try to fight it. George: thanks for taking me off the ice.", George, still shocked by how the situation turned in just a few minutes, looked at him and said: "Don't thank me, kid. If I'd known it would end like this, I would have left you there. Hell, I'd have buried you again." He chuckled grumpily, finally coming somewhat to terms with the resolution of his company's discovery. Then he did something Daniel would have never expected. He extended his hand; Daniel shook it firmly, with a melancholy smile - "You don't happen to have a cigarette, do you?" - Daniel pulled free a cigarette and handed it to George. "So you must be nervous." - "Very.", George replied nervously.

Butch approached the two men with a gesture of his own. "Do you have another, Daniel? I try not to smoke, but this seems like a decent occasion. Besides, I'll be the one who has to fix this whole mess, and I don't see myself doing that without a little stimulation."

George turned to him: "On that note, I'll be expecting

frequent reports on how we should proceed." - "It begins," Butch sighed.

Daniel took a long drag of his own cigarette and thought of Butch weeks from then, buried in paperwork and fighting off all the government offices snooping into the affair. He smiled at them one last time before turning his back to them and boarding an MI6 helicopter with Emily.

He didn't know where he was going, but he knew where he'd been. He knew that he had a lot to teach these people and they a lot to teach him. Even if it's not what Butch and George wanted, it was what the world needed.

ABOUT THE AUTHOR

Antonio M. Calabretta is a Software Engineer living and working in Amsterdam, the Netherlands; since he was a kid he developed a great interest in history, especially in WW2 – related subjects.

Some year ago, he found himself standing in front of a German- built Meteo station at the Imperial War Museum in London, England, and reading the incredible story of this machine, found "somewhere in Greenland" more than 20 years after the war has ended and used by the German Navy to broadcast Meteo conditions to U-Boats so that they knew where to surface and navigate during the night to recharge their batteries.

The project was so secret that when the machine was found it took a while before its real purpose was unveiled: even in Germany nobody knew about them; This posed as a starting point to invent a story explaining some of the WW2 mysteries he avidly read about in the past years, the rest is the story you just read.

Made in the USA
Middletown, DE
15 May 2020